BILL KNOX

◆

ISLE
OF
DRAGONS

Complete and Unabridged

LINFORD
Leicester

First published in Great Britain

Originally published under the name of
Robert MacLeod

First Linford Edition
published 1997

British Library CIP Data

Knox, Bill, *1928* –
    Isle of dragons.—Large print ed.—
    Linford mystery library
    1. Detective and mystery stories
    2. Large type books
    I. Title II. MacLeod, Robert, *1928* –
    823.9'14 [F]

    ISBN 0–7089–5067–1

Published by
F. A. Thorpe (Publishing) Ltd.
Anstey, Leicestershire

Set by Words & Graphics Ltd.
Anstey, Leicestershire
Printed and bound in Great Britain by
T. J. International Ltd., Padstow, Cornwall

This book is printed on acid-free paper

ISLE OF DRAGONS

Talos Cord, the UN Field Reconnaissance trouble-shooter, is ordered to Indonesian Borneo to investigate a rumour which links a Peking-inspired uprising with the promotion of the legend surrounding a long-dead bandit hero. He finds the threat of a bloodbath all too real. The flashpoint is to be a strange, ritual dance to be held on the Isle of Dragons — and that flashpoint is reached before Talos Cord takes the only gamble left to him to prevent disaster.

For Cam

1

THERE were many like the *Tari* on the Borneo trade, tired, overworked little coastal steamers with just enough piston-slapping life remaining to make them profitable. Rust had eaten most of the paintwork on her iron hull and the single funnel aft bore several blatant patches. She lay alongside Tawau harbour, still loading, her sunbaked main deck a disorder of half-stowed cargo and patient, squatting passengers.

Standing at a window on the second floor of the Rajah-Laut Agencies office, Talos Cord switched his attention to the rest of the scene. Tawau's harbour was one of the very few worth mentioning along the whole ragged south-east sweep of the North Borneo coastline, and business seemed brisk. Tear-shaped

1

native *kumpits*, schooners and the rest queued along its length close to vast rafts of timber floated down-river from the interior. Off shore, a couple of sleek Australian cargo ships lay at anchor, waiting their tonnage of copra.

Still further out, across the vast stretch of Sibuko Bay, he could make out the dark green jungle haze which marked the start of Indonesian territory — his final destination, one that somehow created its own wry foreboding.

"Well, what do you think of her?" The gruff, faintly amused voice made Cord turn.

The man seated at the broad steel and chrome desk was plump, bald and in his fifties. White shirt immaculately fresh, sober grey tie carefully knotted, Rajah-Laut's district manager kept efficiency and comfort nicely teamed. Jameson Taggart's office furnishings were functionally modern, and an air conditioner hummed in one corner, battling against the outside temperature.

"The *Tari*?" A twist of a grin creased across Cord's young, bronzed face, to halt, lop-sided, at the old hairline scar which curved across his left cheek. Less than an hour had passed since he'd arrived at Tawau from Jesselton, in the west, aboard a hastily chartered Fokker of doubtful vintage. After that afternoon's flight, even a coastal steamer might have charms. "She's no ocean greyhound, but she'll do. When does she sail?"

"Only when they can't cram anything else aboard. You've plenty of time."

Cord stayed at the window. Down below, on the dusty road leading to the dockside, a heavy truck was edging its way through a heedless bustle of humanity. Malays and Chinese, black-clothed Dusuns, small, slightly built Muruts from the interior, turbanned Sikhs and the rest seemed to make it a point of honour to ignore the truck's bare-chested, cursing, horn-blasting driver until the last possible moment.

3

"Come and finish your drink, man," invited Taggart. "Real liquor's in short supply where you're going."

The whisky glass, ice cubes slowly melting, glinted cool and inviting on its small table. Talos Cord willingly lowered himself into the rattan chair placed beside it and let himself relax. Three days earlier he had been in West Berlin. Berlin in early July had been warm and pleasant. Borneo, what he'd seen of it so far, seemed equally composed of heat, humidity, and the rancid, oily odour of drying copra.

Yet it was in Berlin that the story had first popped up. The deliberate, planted hint that major rebellion was being carefully engineered in an isolated corner of Indonesian Borneo, trouble likely to endanger the uneasy peace of the whole vast island and perhaps infect its neighbours.

Why Soviet Intelligence should choose Berlin for this particular East-West leak, whether the motive was ideological or just plain vindictive, were matters by the way. What mattered was that the Chinese Communists had already gone through one major, bloody setback when they'd attempted a coup in Indonesia. If they were planning to try again, even on a limited scale, Moscow wouldn't be unhappy to see this particular exercise in Peking expansion come unstuck . . . as long as the blame wasn't laid at Moscow's door.

"Well now . . . " slightly annoyed at his guest's silence, Taggart noisily cleared his throat. "The *Tari* can make seven knots with the boiler safety valve screwed down, so it'll be sometime after dawn tomorrow before you get down to Barumma." A touch of embarrassment crossed his face at the need to put his position in words. "I've organised what I can, though there are limits. Rajah-Laut's a strictly commercial trading concern. I've a board of directors who don't like getting involved in anything to do with politics, whatever the brand. It's bad for business, particularly our kind of business."

5

Cord sipped his drink and nodded wryly. "But sometimes you feel differently?"

"Sometimes." Taggart inspected his visitor with a thoughtful deliberation.

Clean-shaven, with black hair cut short, Talos Cord was just over medium height and built on compact lines. Slim and muscular beneath the travel-creased fawn jerkin he wore open over a faded blue shirt, twill slacks and soft leather moccasins, he lazed in the chair with apparent unconcern. The face had dark eyes and a strong nose — and that scar of course. On some men, decided Taggart, it might have been an ugly thing. But with Cord it merged with the rest, softened by the wide humorous mouth, contributing to a hunch that the man opposite had already crammed enough into life to satisfy most people.

Somehow reassured, Taggart thawed again. "How's Andy Beck these days?"

"You know him?" Cord nursed the glass, trying not to show surprise.

"I used to, years back. We fought a spell of the Pacific War together, then I lost touch — until now."

"He's healthy enough." And had a long memory, added Cord mentally. With a vague bitterness he knew that it was inevitably typical for fat, untidy Andrew Beck to be able to know someone in just the right place at the right time. "He's my boss, among other things."

Chief of U.N. Field Reconnaissance, with an office high in the slab-sided United Nations Secretariat in New York, Andrew Beck ruled beside three desk telephones and a world map. He gathered rumours and whispers, hints and jealousies, wove them together, then predicted. Which was why he'd thrust Cord first to Berlin and now to Borneo.

'Peacemakers' was a term sometimes used by people who knew about Field Reconnaissance, and when Beck made a move, sliding one of his men into a situation like a fresh chip in the

7

international poker game, he demanded results. Field Reconnaissance had to report the truth then take local action, drastic or otherwise, to bring down the temperature in whatever conflict was simmering.

One chip added to the heap at the right moment could alter any game — that was Beck's gospel, with a supreme disregard for the nations or problems involved. And surprise was the only wild card he possessed to back his play.

"Ever been in Borneo before?"

Taggart's question brought him back sharply to the present. He shook his head. "Other islands round about, but never here. I've got enough of the language to avoid getting lost."

Despite the air conditioning, Taggart's bald head showed a slight glint of perspiration. The Rajah-Laut manager wiped a handkerchief across the offending area. "Well, I'll take it you know the basic situation. North Borneo is in the Malaysian Federation.

Indonesia has the south and wants the lot. Sukarno tried it with his 'confrontation' war because among other things it took his people's minds off the chaos in their own backyard. Then the Communists tried to take over in Indonesia, got the worst of a two-way massacre, and things cooled down. The confrontation was swept under the carpet. But that doesn't mean it's been forgotten — or that the local military are likely to welcome a U.N. agent."

Cord's eyes twinkled at the tacit understatement. Indonesia had carved a little place in history as the first nation to quit the United Nations. Most members would have preferred her to stay, and had been relieved when she finally returned to the fold. The more cynical murmured privately that it was always better to have a potentially rowdy neighbour where you could keep an eye on things, rather than have him running around loose outside.

9

"I've a passport which says I'm a photographer," he reminded. "The story is I'm working for a European magazine group, doing a picture series on twentieth-century Borneo."

"So I gathered," agreed Taggart dryly. "Well, when you're down there remember they've rechristened Borneo — it's now Kalimantan." He opened a drawer of the desk, brought out an envelope, and pushed it across. "Whatever credentials you've got, this will back them up. Personal letter from me to Colonel Suramo, military governor for Barumma district. If he likes you, everything's fine. If he doesn't, that's your problem."

"Thanks." Cord opened the envelope and glanced at the single typed sheet it contained.

"It says you came to us for help and that I'm passing you on to him," said Taggart neutrally. "It doesn't say I know you or that Rajah-Laut is backing you. But Suramo has — well —a personal arrangement with us, so any introduction should carry some weight."

"Business is business?" Cord gave a satisfied chuckle, slipped the letter back in its envelope, and tucked it away. "I'd like to hear more about the colonel."

"Someone else can do that." Taggart pressed a button at his elbow. In a moment, there was a soft tap on the office door and a slim, honey-bronze Malay girl, pert in a European cotton dress and high-heeled sandals, entered the room. "Mora, is Peter Dimo here yet?"

"He waits outside, *tuan*." Her eyes strayed towards Cord for a moment. "You want him now?"

"Yes." As the girl went out, Taggart turned back to Cord. "Peter Dimo's on our payroll as a purchase agent — which in his case means being contact man for most of the coast around Barumma. He's part Malay, part Chinese and probably a few other things. He drifted down to us from

Singapore, and every other week I wish he'd drift straight back again."

"The independent type?"

"That's one way of putting it." Taggart sighed a little. "Still, he knows the right people, where to bribe, how much, and when. He'll go down with you on the *Tari*, and I've asked him to show you around a little. But I want one thing understood." He leaned forward, spreading both hands wide on the desk top. "Don't involve him in anything. Dimo's the reason why we handle so much of the copra and rubber trade coming out of the south. He's too valuable for us to risk losing."

"I'll try to remember," murmured Cord soothingly. "How much does he know about it all?"

"I've told him you're a photographer. If he thinks differently, he'll keep it to himself." Taggart chewed unhappily on his lower lip. "Cord, nobody's bothered to even hint to me what's going on. Now, when I'm helping . . . "

"Sorry." Cord gave a slow, good-humoured shake of his head. "Andrew Beck wants a job done and I'm here to do it. Call me awkward if you want, but that's how it is."

Taggart growled to himself, then swung round in his chair as a brisk, confident rap sounded on the door. "*Masuk* . . . come in, Peter."

The tall, bean-pole thin individual who entered was very different from anything Talos Cord had anticipated. Peter Dimo was still in his early twenties, with a mop of dark, heavily oiled hair. He wore a cream linen suit, the jacket at least one size too wide for his slender frame, highly polished light tan shoes which almost matched his complexion, and heavy, thick-lensed spectacles which couldn't quite disguise the speculative interest on his thin, oddly boyish face.

"*Selamat siang* . . . good afternoon, Jameson." The voice was a light, almost accentless tenor. "So this is your Mr Cord?"

13

Taggart nodded. "I've been telling him about you."

"And now I've got to live up to the description?" Dimo used a forefinger to push the spectacles a little higher on his nose and grinned. "I don't know much about photography, Mr Cord, except maybe the naughty pictures smuggled in from Hong Kong. The police have one fantastic collection." He brought a small, ornate silver cigarette case from one pocket and thumbed it open. "They're American . . . "

"No thanks." Cord rose from his chair but shook his head and fished out one of the thick, black cheroots he kept in the top pocket of his jerkin. "I only use these." He glanced inquiringly towards Taggart.

"Jameson's vices are restricted," declared Dimo. He struck a match, waited until Cord had the cheroot glowing, then lit a cigarette and drew on it with a delicate precision. "I've checked on the *Tari*. She's about ready to leave."

"Good." Taggart was relieved. "Peter, when you see Colonel Suramo . . ."

"I will talk to him like a brother," agreed Dimo. For Cord's benefit, he explained. "The colonel controls export permits from Barumma. Each native boat must have a permit before it can bring a cargo here, and permits have been strangely sticky the last couple of weeks."

"So the colonel will have to be made happy again?" queried Cord.

"Maybe." Dimo gave a grimace which made him look younger than ever. "When you get to him with your cameras, for instance, it might help if you suggested you'd like to do a special portrait study."

"Might help who? Me, or Rajah-Laut?"

"Let's say everyone," grunted Taggart, rising to his feet. "One last thing, Cord. If there's any minor awkwardness on the *Tari*, leave it to Peter to sort out. He knows the ropes, you don't."

"He's more than welcome." Cord

15

held out his hand. "Thanks for your help, Taggart."

"Save that till you get back," said Taggart sombrely. He shook hands briefly. "Safe journey."

"Let's go, then," suggested Dimo cheerfully.

Taggart gave a brief, absent wave of his hand as they left. Then, as the door closed and he was left alone, he sank back into his chair, frowning. If any kind of trouble was due to flare in the south the whole Indonesian copra supply would dry up. The dried white coconut meat, its rich food-oil content so much in demand, would immediately rise in price on the world markets. Supposing head office took a few outside options on some additional non-Indonesian lots and hung on to already warehoused shipments until the market reacted to the inevitable law of supply and demand . . .

Mind made up, he reached for the telephone.

Talos Cord's green canvas travel bag was lying in the main downstairs office, where a dozen or so clerks and typists, most of them Chinese, were hard at work. Peter Dimo excused himself briefly and returned dragging a suitcase which seemed to weigh down his tall, scrawny frame.

"Ready now," he announced. "It shouldn't be too bad a trip — I fixed us a cabin. Oh, and call me Peter, huh?"

Outside the main door, the afternoon heat hit them like a solid wall. Dimo glanced around and beckoned. A burly Dusun porter in greasy shorts, a faded sweatband round his broad forehead, came over from the wall where he'd been lounging. He nodded at Dimo's instruction, took the case as if it was a feather and reached for Cord's bag.

"No." Cord shook his head. "*Tidak*."

The man shrugged, hefted Dimo's case, and set off towards the dock.

"It would have been safe enough," murmured Dimo. "Crime around here is plain, honest violence — Tawau people are just beginning to learn how to steal."

"I was thinking of my cameras," explained Cord. "I don't want them thumped around."

"I forgot." Something in the tenor voice made Cord glance sharply. But the gaze which met his own was mild and innocent. "To a photographer, of course, cameras are important."

They followed the padding Dusun through the crowded street, passing a noisy cluster of makeshift market stalls where dried, high-smelling fish vied for custom with vegetables from inland and gaily decorated pottery. Two cane baskets slung from her shoulders by a yoke, an old woman in black ankle-length skirts scowled as she bumped into Cord. Next moment the scowl changed to a leathery grin as Dimo murmured something in her ear.

"What was the password?" asked

Cord as they moved on. Dimo chuckled blithely. "I told her you were a poor *tuan* who'd been drinking too much. Perhaps she believed it, perhaps not — but it made her happier."

Things were quieter once they reached the dock gate. A solitary Malay constable, rifle slung over one shoulder, nodded lazily as they passed through then lapsed back into his previous sleepy-eyed state.

"There's something else I'd like to know." Cord switched the weight of his bag from one hand to the other, already feeling his shirt sticky with perspiration in the oppressing heat. "What did Jameson Taggart mean about, 'minor awkwardnesses' on the *Tari*?"

"That?" Dimo shrugged a little. "Perhaps just the cockroaches, a prize breed." He became more serious. "Or maybe he was thinking of the *orang-laut* — the Bajaus, our sea gypsies. Like that one." He thumbed briefly in the direction of a squat, brawny figure standing beside a mound of packing cases just ahead. Muscular frame and colour of copper, a dirty, flat turban wrapped tightly around his head, naked to the waist, the man had his thumbs tucked into the broad ex-army webbing belt which supported his salt-faded pantaloons. His jaws chewed slowly and rhythmically. As they passed, he grinned insolently and spat. A stream of red betel juice landed scant inches from their feet.

"Typical," said Dimo ruefully. "They live on the sea and from the sea. They may be fishermen one night and pirates the next." He sensed Cord's unspoken scepticism. "Not comical characters, Mr Cord, but the kind who use powerboats and automatic weapons."

"I've heard of them," admitted Cord. "More than one U.N. agency report described the triangle of water formed by the southern Philippines, Borneo and Celebes as a nest of raiding violence one stage short of anarchy."

"Then you maybe know they usually concentrate on hi-jacking smuggled cargoes. Cigarettes, silks, maybe liquor — small bulk, high value stuff. Occasionally, they capture a village and gut it of anything worth money. Normally, regular coastal shipping isn't troubled, but right now they've gone sensitive." One long, bony hand fluttered unhappily. "Last month three boatloads strayed too far north and met a British frigate. They were captured, and this makes the rest ill-tempered."

"But doesn't the *Tari* carry an escort?"

Dimo shook his head.

"Nice to know," Cord thanked him dryly. "And I thought you said people around here were the honest type."

Behind the thick spectacle lenses, Dimo blinked. "I meant it. But the *orang-laut* are different — for some of them piracy is family tradition stuff, a way of life." He decided it was time to be reassuring. "Nothing's likely to happen. Even if it does, they're more interested in loot than blood."

The porter had stopped at the top

of the narrow gangway leading down to the *Tari*. Dimo handed him a coin, took the suitcase, and the man wandered off. Cord's eyes were on the coaster. She was about a hundred and fifty feet long, probably about two hundred tons, a long time had passed since her decks had been hosed and even longer since any part of her had known a paintbrush. The few crewmen working aboard were as sullen a bunch of layabouts as he could remember.

"So she's not the Borneo-Hilton," confessed Dimo, reading his thoughts. "But she floats and she gets there." His thin face split in a grin. "Most times anyway. Let's claim that cabin."

He led the way, struggling down the gangway with his case. Cord followed him aft, squeezing past the knots of deck passengers until at last they entered a narrow, stale-smelling companionway. Dimo dumped his case outside the second door along and waved an invitation. Cord twisted the handle, swung open the door, then his mouth fell open.

The cabin was small, little more than two bunks, a locker and some floor-space. The snub-nosed, raven-haired Indonesian girl who stared down at him from the top bunk was too surprised to speak. The lower bunk's threadbare blanket was covered in a scatter of discarded clothing and standing beside it, halfway through pulling on a green shirt-blouse, stood a slim, freckle-faced redhead. She showed a fascinating area of firm, tanned midriff between bra and belt-line, and at that moment she had the most angry green eyes Cord had known.

"Get out!" She flushed and snatched the shirt's front round her. The girl on the top bunk came to life with an indignant squeal and began scrambling down, pleated nylon skirt riding high on plump, well-shaped thighs.

"Sorry," began Cord. "But . . ."

"Out!" The door slammed shut in his face.

Cord gave a soft, appreciative whistle. Prospects aboard the coaster had certainly taken on a new dimension. At his side, Peter Dimo solemnly removed his spectacles and chewed thoughtfully at one leg of the frame, grinning.

"*Hai* . . . the ladies seem annoyed!"

"And probably dangerous." Cord shifted grip on his bag once more. "Looks like we came to the wrong cabin."

"No, this is the only one for passengers." Dimo replaced his glasses, leaned forward, and tapped hopefully on the door. "Hello, in there. If we could — ah — speak to you when you're ready . . . "

"Stay where you are," firmly warned the redhead's voice. Quick, scuttling noises came from the other side of the door, then at last it swung open.

"Well?" She stood determinedly in the doorway, fists clenched by her side. The shirt had been tucked tightly into a pair of bleached cotton slacks, the debris of clothing had disappeared, and

24

the other girl waited inches behind her, equally ready to repel invasion.

Dimo cleared his throat. "Ah . . . my name is Peter Dimo, and this is Mr Cord . . . "

"Who doesn't knock on doors," snapped the redhead.

"Don't you ever lock them?" countered Cord, raising a quizzical eyebrow.

"I did, but . . . but . . . " Her mouth tightening, she grabbed the outer handle and twisted it back and forward. "The damn thing somehow still opens from the outside. How were we to know?"

"Unfortunate," agreed Dimo sympathetically. "But equally unfortunate, there has been some mistake. This is our cabin."

"*Kamu gila* . . . are you crazy or something?" The other girl's words came tumbling out, bubbling with indignation. A long strand of her raven-black hair had come loose and had fallen across her forehead. Impatiently, she brushed it back. "You long, miserable *lalat*! This is our cabin, and we can prove it. See for yourself." She brandished a slip of paper under their eyes. "This is our receipt. Cabin A — correct?"

"Correct, little one. But . . . " a glint of sudden understanding in his eyes, Dimo carefully produced the slip's twin from one pocket. "Bingo! This is also for Cabin A. The only difference is yours seems to have cost ten dollars more. And unfortunately, there's no Cabin B." He gave a flop-shouldered shrug towards Cord. "I forgot to mention that our captain is notoriously underpaid."

The redhead exchanged a startled glance with her companion then swallowed, still defiant. "Well, that's your problem. We're not moving."

"I'd a feeling you might say that," mused Cord, grinning.

"Then that's that." Her mouth tightened again. "And you can tell that bandit up top we'll be along to get

26

some of our money back. Goodbye."
The door closed firmly again.

Dimo sucked hard on his teeth, stooped, and lifted his suitcase. "My old father had three wives," he said bitterly. "Never argue with a woman, he used to tell me — and Mr Cord, just this once I'm going to be a dutiful son."

★ ★ ★

The *Tari*'s captain was a wary-eyed, fat Indonesian whose sole symbol of authority was the gold-braided cap balanced precariously on his head. And, for the moment, he was busy. Before they could get to him the coaster had cast off and was thumping a noisy way out into Sibuko Bay. The sea was calm, the wind almost non-existent, and the deck passengers had already begun settling beside their little bundles of luggage. One group of half a dozen, a family party of Chinese, were calmly erecting a miniature shelter of mats beneath a lifeboat near the stern.

Cord waited below the bridge, watching the blue water slip lazily by, leaving Peter Dimo to handle things. Finally, when the tall, bespectacled Malaysian reappeared, he was with the *Tari*'s mate. Scowling, the man gestured them to follow him and headed aft. He stopped by a cabin door, threw it open, and disappeared inside. At last, the mate emerged clutching a hastily filled kitbag, thumbed over his shoulder, and stumped off without a word.

"His?" queried Cord.

"Uh-huh. Orders." Dimo's confidence was back to its usual. "I told the captain that otherwise you'd take his picture and let the world know he was a chiselling crook."

They went in. The mate's quarters were even smaller than the other cabin, and what looked suspiciously like the trunk of an engine-room exhaust duct bulged above the single bunk. When Cord touched it, his fingers felt as if they'd been blistered. Empty beer cans were piled inside a wire waste basket, a battered armchair might have been salvaged from some garbage dump, and the other furnishings were as old and faded and uninspiring as the pin-ups on the walls. From the look of things, he began to envy the deck travellers.

"The bunk is yours, the chair mine . . . " Dimo refused to listen to protests. "But, first a small precaution." He opened the suitcase, rummaged inside, and produced an aerosol tin of insecticide. For the next few moments he moved busily around, spraying liberally, until the bug killer's highly perfumed odour reeked throughout the cabin. At last, finished, he dumped the emptied tin, peeled off his jacket, and flopped happily into the armchair. "Cameras okay?"

"Fine." Cord had already been checking. He dumped the two cameras on the bunk's blanket. One was a 35 mil. Leica, the other a large Japanese twin reflex. He'd bought both second-hand to make sure of having equipment which looked well used. "Maybe I'll take a few shots while we're aboard. Atmosphere stuff."

"Atmosphere we have," agreed Dimo. "Got plenty of film?"

"Enough." It was in two large sealed tins and most of the contents in each were genuine. He sat on the bunk and found it ominously lumpy and uneven. "What about Barumma, Peter? I'd like to hear about the place from an expert."

"That depends on what you want to know — as a photographer." Dimo eyed him strangely for a moment, then made a ritual of lighting a cigarette.

"Meaning?"

"Nothing that matters. I have a built-in resistance to curiosity." Deliberately Dimo changed the subject. "Anyway, more important, I found out a little about those girls."

"Well?" Cord let it pass.

"The little dark one's name is

30

Sadiah — Sadiah Beh." Dimo rubbed his smooth, slightly pointed chin appreciatively. "*Wah* . . . and a fiery little one she is too! The one with the red hair and determination is Katherine Shellon — her friends call her Kate. They are, of all things, from some Manila museum. But I didn't have time to ask why."

"You got this from the captain?"

"From the little one, Sadiah." Dimo stretched his long legs happily. "We had a talk while we waited for our captain. She was along to get their ten dollars back — and she managed it!"

"That figures." For a moment, Cord imagined the scene. Then casually, he tried again. "Now, how about Barumma?"

"Back to work." Dimo sighed disapproval. "There's Barumma town, and then the district — Kalimantan is a patchwork of districts, with the army running most of them. Colonel Kaan Suramo is boss as far as Barumma is concerned, with no

31

one to challenge him — except when Central Government occasionally sends some official from Djakarta to inspect the books and guess at what's really going on."

"And Suramo?"

"A big frog in a small pool and conscious of it both ways." The schoolboy grin held a slight touch of derision. "He's no worse than some of the others and wiser than most. Suramo prefers appreciations paid in American dollars. The Indonesian rupiah is too delicate in health for his liking."

Cord nodded his understanding. "Which means he doesn't intend trying to collect any pension for long service and good conduct. Peter, my briefing on Barumma district was that there's a couple of hundred miles of territory, plus some off-shore islands. And that there's a hefty copra trade, some rice and rubber, and a lot of army — plus a few diamond workings near the coast."

"A few?" Dimo's voice quivered

slightly. "There you have an under-statement. Borneo diamonds are one of the few things that keeps Indonesia from going bankrupt. And in Borneo, some of the best diamonds happen to come out of Barumma."

"Which pleases Colonel Suramo?"

"Which upsets him very much," corrected Dimo. "The main diamond pits are on Kuwa, an island just off shore — and Central Government has them under direct control. Even the capital knows better than to lay too much temptation in one man's lap, so they keep a full company of Javanese infantry as a permanent guard on Kuwa. The Javanese are disliked by most people as outsiders — but Suramo sees them as the enemy, robbing him of his rightful prey."

"Well, he can't win them all." Cord made a show of turning his attention to the cameras, tinkering with their focusing. Most of what Dimo had said fitted, without taking him further forward. Colonel Suramo had been part of the story Field Reconnaissance had received, the only name actually mentioned — though it had been made plain he wasn't the top man in what was being organised.

But Andrew Beck's final, cabled briefing had offered up another name, one with a riddle attached. Seventy years back a troublesome Borneo chieftain known as Tan Sallong had been blown to bits by a mountain gun while raiding British administered territory. As a result, he had a shaky place in Borneo's history as an early revolutionary hero.

Over the last few months someone in Indonesia had begun a quiet, skilful public relations job aimed at burnishing up the long-dead rebel's reputation. One suggestion had been he should feature on a special issue postage stamp for Kalimantan — though Djakarta, suspicious of regional heroes, had turned it down. More recently, Kalimantan's radio stations had begun playing a new song which amounted to a ballad in his praise — mostly on record request programmes. There were stories of newly formed Tan Sallong study groups.

One resurrected revolutionary, one graft-happy colonel — well, they made an unorthodox team. Cord toyed with the Leica, swung it idly up to eye level, caught Peter Dimo's face in the viewing frame, and clicked the shutter.

"*Tjelaka* . . . cut that out!" The lanky youngster exploded up from the chair, his thin face tense and suddenly sallow. "Keep that thing away from me."

"What's the panic?" Cord swung himself upright, as much puzzled as amazed. "There's no film in them yet!"

Dimo swallowed hard, the Adam's apple bobbing on his scrawny neck. He moistened his lips and forced an approximation of a laugh. "Maybe it's the native in me — white man's box have-um evil eye. I just don't want to be in any of your pictures. Okay?"

35

"If that's how you want it." Slowly, wooden-faced, Cord broke open the back of the camera and held it up. "Empty. Satisfied?"

Embarrassed now, Dimo nodded. "All right, so now I start apologising." He looked away for a moment, dropped his cigarette, and ground it methodically under one heel. When he turned again, his manner was back to normal. "Look, suppose you load that camera and use the last of decent daylight on deck. Then we can eat." One foot tapped the suitcase. "It's all in here — another rule on the *Tari*. Bring your own food. The captain's table doesn't rise much above rice and dried fish."

"I'll take a look around." Cord collected a loose cassette of film from his bag, slung the Leica's strap over one shoulder, then stopped halfway to the door. "Peter, there's a name I got from someone on the way to Tawau. Ever hear of an oldtime bandit called Tan Sallong?"

"No, sorry." Dimo shook his dark

36

mop of hair. "That one doesn't register."

But the denial had been a little too quick, too positive, decided Cord. Like the episode with the camera and the rest, it helped add up to the fact that Peter Dimo had some secrets of his own. Thoughtfully, Cord went out and closed the door behind him. As an ally, Dimo could be an asset. In opposition, he might be a particularly troublesome factor.

★ ★ ★

The wind had risen a little and the coaster's blunt bows were taking an occasional drenching of spray. Enjoying it, deliberately forgetting his problems for the moment, Talos Cord took his time wandering around the plodding vessel's swaying decks. A dozen frames of the Leica's film soon used, he found the deck passengers and crew paid little attention to his exploring. Most of the cargo was merchandise goods, cases of instant coffee piled side by side with vehicle spares and cartons of detergent.

They were still in sight of land when he finally returned to the cabin. His fingers on the door handle, he stopped as a high, protesting tinkle of laughter came from inside, followed by Dimo's softer chuckle. Cord grinned, knocked, and the door opened after a moment's delay. The raven-haired Indonesian girl brushed past him with a quick smile and headed aft along the deck.

Cord went in, closed the door, and looked around. "Well? Don't tell me she looked in to borrow a cup of sugar."

"Something like that, I suppose." Dimo's eyes twinkled behind the spectacles. "Still, everything's ready."

A small table in one corner of the cabin held cups, a Thermos of coffee and two plastic plates. A tiny spirit stove purred a blue flame on the floor, heating a pot filled with a simmering curry.

"The tin-opener was a wonderful invention." Dimo turned away, rummaged in the suitcase again, and produced a bottle. "Like a spot of this first?"

"Whisky?" Cord blinked, beginning to understand why that suitcase had been so heavy. "Where . . ."

"From Jameson Taggart's stock, though he doesn't know it. Let's say with the compliments of Rajah-Laut."

They ate in comparative silence, talked a little over a second drink from the bottle, and when Cord next looked out of the grimy porthole it was velvet dark outside, the moon high in the sky, the *Tari*'s engine still thumping the same monotonous rhythm. He lit a cheroot and glanced towards Dimo.

"Feel like a walk around?"

"Me?" Dimo shook his head. "I've some paperwork to organise. Little details to have ready for Colonel Suramo's attention."

Cord left him to it, went out on deck, and leaned against a rail for a spell, smoking quietly, glad to escape from the cabin's oven-like dimensions. The moon's glow on the night sea was edged with black where the distant coastline began. Midway, a cluster of lights marked a group of fishing boats at work. Near the *Tari*'s stern, a frayed glow escaped round the edges of the Chinese family's shelter. A transistor radio was squawking from somewhere close.

It wasn't often he had the chance to feel so peacefully content. Tomorrow might be different, but he'd take things as they came. That was one lesson he'd learned early enough, even before Andrew Beck and Field Reconnaissance.

A vague figure moved near the coaster's bow. Cord watched idly for a moment then suddenly grinned and tossed the remains of the cheroot over the side. As its red glow died on impact he headed for'ard, stepping carefully over a snoring figure wrapped in what looked like a vast, hairy blanket.

Katherine Shellon was still standing

near the port bow, a dark suède jacket over her shoulders, the faint breeze ruffling her shoulder-length hair, her eyes on the water. She didn't hear him approach until he was about a yard away, and when she turned her expression changed to an immediate mixture of cool wariness and embarrassed recollection.

"How's the cabin?" Cord stopped beside her, back to the rail, hands in pockets, a friendly twinkle in his eyes.

"A place to sleep, but not much more," she admitted ruefully. "I heard you managed to fix up something."

"The bridal suite." Cord eased himself up a little from the rail. "You know, last time we didn't quite get round to proper introductions . . ."

In the moonlight it was difficult to be certain. But he could have sworn there was a hint of laughter in the set of her mouth. "Let's call it an awkward moment worth forgetting," she suggested, her voice low and clear. "I'm . . ."

41

"Kate Shellon — I know. My travelling expert got the details."

She laughed, a soft chuckle, taking a pack of cigarettes from her jacket. "So did mine. I expected to see you carrying a camera."

"Right now I'm off duty." He produced his lighter, flicked it to life, and held the flame sheltered between his cupped hands. Her head bent towards it, a faint wisp of sandalwood perfume reaching his nostrils. The lips holding the cigarette were wide and soft, the nose above short and straight. He'd come across more beautiful women, but this one carried an indefinable quality of her own. The cigarette lit, she leaned back and he said, "One thing Peter didn't discover is why you're here, Kate. All he knew was you're from some museum in Manila."

"Which makes me sound like a Ming vase or a stuffed elephant. Well, it's a long story . . ."

"But I've no pressing engagements."

"No, that's true." She nodded solemn

agreement. "Well, the museum's by the way and its real title is the State Department of Ethnic Studies. About a year ago, back home . . . "

"England?" He didn't think so. There was something else in the voice.

"Melbourne now. My folks emigrated about ten years back. Anyway, I was there doing a post-graduate thing on an ethnic study of Pacific cultures — which involves taking island folk-lore, separating fact from fiction, building up something resembling racial history from the results. I landed a special scholarship grant, and that got me out to Manila."

Cord murmured his appreciation. "Which means you must be pretty good."

"Or lucky. But since then I've been working with a tape recorder around the Philippines, gathering material — and now I'm trying down here, to see how some of the legends have altered with inter-island migrations." She frowned a

43

little. "Did you know they've got their own version of the story of Adam and Eve, something that's remarkably like Noah and the Flood, and a whole lot more?"

"I'll take your word for it." He looked past her for a moment. Another boat was coming up from the south, still too far distant for it to be more than a vague shape and a masthead light. "Has Sadiah been with you all the time?"

Kate Shellon shook her head. "No. She's still a final year student at Manila. But she's keen, she knows every tape recording technique there is, and she helped a lot getting us the permits to work down here."

"You make it sound like there were problems."

"Problems?" She gave a shudder. "Too right there were. I want Barumma on my list because when the Dutch ran things they rated it one place where the villages really kept up a lot of the old customs. My first permit application

44

went off six months back. The official okay finally came through three weeks ago. We're getting here only just in time for one annual festival I really want to collect. If it hadn't been for Sadiah finding us some sponsors in Barumma . . ."

"Sponsors?" He picked up interest.

"A local group who're interested in the same kind of thing. They call themselves the Tan Sallong Society."

He hid his surprise with an effort and kept his voice level. "Well, you're ahead of me. My nearest thing to a contact is an introduction to the local top man, Colonel Suramo."

"Then we'll see more of each other," she declared. "Sadiah got our permits through him — he's one of the study group."

Cord digested the information without comment. "What about this Tan Sallong character — does he interest you?"

"No, he's more or less modern. Anything I want goes back a long way — the theory is the main Borneo tribes started off from mainland China and took about a thousand years or so to get here." She flicked her cigarette over the side and looked across the water. "I want the stories that have gone down father-to-son, mother-to-daughter, about how things all began, how they crossed the sea — maybe in boats not much different from that one."

Cord nodded. The craft he'd noticed earlier was coming close now. It was a big black *kumpit*, with a single, vast leg-of-mutton sail. Probably it was on a copra run up to Tawau. The moonlight was strong enough for him to be able to pick out a man standing at her bow, waving.

At his side, Kate Shellon sighed. "That sort of thing sometimes makes me envy people here — if you forget the rest."

"The simple life?" Cord watched the boat. A faint wash of phosphorescence rippled out from her bow, a starker white against the silvered sea. Captured in oils, the picture would have been a star exhibit in any gallery. "Fine, but think of . . ." he stopped, instincts jangling an alarm.

The *kumpit*'s lateen sail had come tumbling down. The bark of a powerful engine starting up was followed by the rhythmic pulse-beat of twin exhausts. Gathering speed, the vessel began curving in towards the *Tari*. He looked round. The light from the Chinese family's shelter had disappeared. The transistor had stopped playing. Someone on the coaster's bridge was shouting orders.

"What's wrong?" Kate Shellon looked at him, puzzled.

"I've a feeling . . ." he didn't finish. The harsh glare of a spotlight lanced across the water from the *kumpit*'s bow. He sensed as much as saw vague shapes moving behind it. "Down, Kate!"

"But . . ."

"Now." One arm around her waist, he pulled her flat on the deck, holding her down. The harsh, barking staccato

47

of a heavy machine-gun tore the night. A long burst of tracer headed with deceptive laziness towards the *Tari* then whip-lashed across her bow. The spotlight's beam steadied on the coaster's bridge and another burst of tracer hosepiped over, high again, slashing at her radio mast and funnel.

No further invitation was needed. The bridge telegraph pealed and the *Tari*'s engine died. In the sudden silence, while she lost way, someone began wailing.

Grimly, Cord rose up and helped the redhead to her feet.

"All right?"

She nodded, her face pale. "Yes — and thanks."

The coaster had become stationary, rolling gently in the waves. Footsteps hurrying along the deck made him turn. Peter Dimo's lanky figure came hastily towards them.

"You okay, Mr Cord?" He showed relief. "Well, that's something."

"It helps," agreed Cord soberly. He

realised he still had his arm round the girl. Her body, a corner of his mind registered, was warm and firm. "Who are they?"

Peter Dimo looked out at the *kumpit*, now coming alongside in smoothly efficient style. A squad of men were waiting on her deck, and the tripod-mounted machine gun near her bow was still trained menacingly on the coaster's bridge.

"Visitors, Mr Cord." He ran a long, thin hand through his thatch of hair. "*Orang-laut* pirates. Jameson Taggart would make a good prophet." He turned to the girl. "Miss Shellon, I think we better find Sadiah before she worries more. Then we do nothing — just wait." He hesitated, his mouth twisting strangely yet reassuringly. "Why they are here should not concern you."

2

SADIAH was already searching on her own. They saw her a moment later, caught in the glare of the *Kumpit*'s spotlight, standing as if bewildered just below the *Tari*'s bridge, a white silk scarf covering her raven hair. Dimo forced his way through the milling knots of panicking deck passengers and brought her back.

"Kate — " she gave a quick sigh of relief as she saw her friend " — after the shooting, I thought . . . " her voice died away as the *kumpit* bumped alongside. Then, biting her lip, she asked, "What should we do?"

"Nothing," said Cord firmly and swiftly. Men were already swarming aboard from the *kumpit*, and by their looks it was no time for popgun heroics. "Just stay where we are, move when we're told, and play the rest by ear."

There were at least a dozen in the boarding party, men clad in what looked like old army fatigue overalls dyed a dark green with matching headcloths. A few had automatic carbines, the rest carried rifles with grenades pouched at their waists, and they fanned out with a smooth precision. Their leader, a broad-shouldered figure with a carbine cradled under one arm, shouted an order to the boat alongside then signalled his party to begin. As he did, he stepped into the direct light from one of the *Tari*'s decklamps.

Kate Shellon gasped. Where the face should have been was a smooth, featureless veil of gauze, broken only by two small eyeslits.

"I know them now." Peter Dimo spoke close to Cord's ear, his voice flat and colourless.

"A tough bunch?" Already, two of the raiders had reached the coaster's bridge and the captain and helmsman were being bundled out.

"Yes." Dimo drew a deep, unhappy

breath. "The one with the veil calls himself Captain Muka. Whatever he looks like under that thing, I wish we were a long way from here."

Using kicks and gunbutts freely, the raiders were now rounding up passengers and crew, herding them up towards the bow. One green-clad figure came towards them, a hard, dark face snarled, and the rifle in his hands swung to emphasise the order. They went along like the rest, past the silent, watchful Captain Muka. Two of his men were already posted as guards over the crowded captives. Each had a sub-machine gun — Chinese M.41s with the round drum magazine. Not that it mattered, Cord told himself grimly. Communist gift bundles of weapons were scattered all over the Far East, with no one to say who'd originally owned them.

"*Sekarang dengarkan* . . . " one of the men barked a few short words of warning. Cord caught enough, guessed enough, to know they were being told to stay put or end up dead. Nearby, almost the last arrivals, booted out of their shelter of mats, the Chinese family huddled together for mutual protection. But the wailing and crying had ended. Now they were like the rest — people waiting in a silent, tight-wound tension under the moonlight while the soft background murmur of the sea merged with the gentle creaking of the coaster's ancient deck. And the raiders were still busy, searching the ship with a methodical determination.

"It doesn't fit — it just doesn't fit." Peter Dimo shook his head, puzzled. "Muka doesn't bother with small stuff — and that's what we are."

"You mean they want something special that's aboard?" Kate Shellon moistened her lips. "Then I hope they find it, and soon."

"Something or someone . . ." Dimo broke off as the nearest of their guards strode towards him, scowling. The man's eyes glittered balefully then the sub-machine gun swung, the barrel

53

raking across the Malaysian's forehead, smashing his spectacles, sending him reeling back. With a grunt, the green uniformed figure turned back to his post.

At last there was a shout from below the *Tari*'s bridge. Two of the pirates emerged from a companionway, dragging a small, elderly figure between them. He fell, was pulled upright, tried to struggle, and was quickly clubbed behind the ear. As they watched, the limp captive was hauled down to Captain Muka. The raiders' leader nodded, and the man was bundled towards the coaster's rail like a parcel of dirty washing.

"No!" Kate Shellon started forward. Cord grabbed her arm, holding her back.

"Easy," he said tersely. "They went to enough trouble finding him. They're not going to throw him away." He glanced at Dimo. The tall, thin Malaysian, a broad trickle of blood staining one side of his face, managed a nod of agreement. Sadiah Beh was close beside him, using a wadded handkerchief to mop at the bleeding.

Without ceremony the prisoner was dumped into the waiting *kumpit*. A whistle shrilled and as the rest of the boarding party began to reappear on deck their leader strolled towards the bow, casually inspecting the rest of his catch. He stopped, slung the carbine over one shoulder, and the veiled face, the loose ends of the gauze bundled into the collar of his overalls like a bee-keeper's mask, turned towards Cord.

"*Orang Belanda?*"

"He wants to know if you're Dutch," muttered Dimo. "He's got a reputation for disliking them."

"Then I'd better put him right," said Cord from the corner of his mouth. "I'd hate to be someone's big mistake." He raised his voice. "*Tidak. Orang Inggeris.*"

"English?" The raider showed an immediate interest. "I speak some. Let

55

me see you, Englishman."

Cord shrugged and stepped forward. "Well?"

The veiled figure glanced at the nearest guard and jerked his head. The man obeyed quickly, using one hand to poke the muzzle of his weapon against Cord's stomach while the other searched Cord's pockets. Cord kept his face impassive as his wallet was found and passed back, but sighed a little as the cheroots vanished from the top pocket of his jerkin.

"This is all?" The pirate leader thumbed through the wallet dispassionately then slipped it inside his tunic. "You disappoint me."

"Sorry," apologised Cord dryly. "I'll try and do better next time."

Something like a laugh came from behind the veil. Muka brushed past him then stopped in front of Kate Shellon. "Yours, Englishman?"

"A friend."

"Ah." He saw Sadiah next, sucked admiringly on his teeth, and muttered something in her ear. She turned away angrily and he shrugged, moved on until he'd located the *Tari*'s captain, then shoved that quivering individual on ahead of him towards the bridge.

For another ten long minutes they were kept penned at the bow until a final whistle-blast shrilled. One by one the raiders dropped back aboard the *kumpit*, their leader last to leave. As he did, the boat's engine throbbed to life and in a moment it was drawing away from the *Tari*, curving on a course towards land.

The departure was a signal for pandemonium. Like a miniature wave, the deck passengers scurried to retrieve scattered luggage, leaving the coaster's crew milling around in a noisy, aimless confusion. In the middle of it, Cord realised that Peter Dimo had disappeared with the rest. He cursed softly and aimlessly, watching the *kumpit*'s silhouette gradually disappear into the darkness, the big lateen sail already being hoisted.

"All that for — for one little man."
Kate Shellon came beside him, pale-faced, shaking her head. "What'll they do to him, Talos?"

"Depends who he is — or what he's done," said Cord grimly. "Where's Sadiah?"

"Gone to our cabin to find out the worst." She forced a smile. "I'd better get there too. But whatever's gone, at least we're still in one piece."

He went part-way with her then headed for his own cabin. The door lay open and the light was burning inside. But for the rest — he stood a moment in the doorway, anger smouldering. Someone had taken his travel bag, upended it, and dumped the contents over the floor. Dimo's suitcase lay open too, clothes spilling out. Swiftly, he went down on his knees and began to sort through the debris. The cameras and film boxes were intact. All that appeared missing was a rubber hand-torch and a bone-handled Swedish clasp-knife. He sighed briefly over the latter, then started to clear up.

"That's what I call a mess." Peter Dimo loped into the cabin, lowered himself into the chair, and screwed up his face in disgust. The gash on his forehead still oozed red and blood stained the front of his linen jacket. "It's the same most places. They smashed the radio, took a few cases of cigarettes, and looted a little on the side. But it looks like all they really wanted was the old man."

"Who was he?"

Without the spectacles, Dimo's eyes were mild and watery. He shrugged. "According to our captain, a paying guest he had in his own cabin. Name of Chou Sie, a diamond merchant. He lives in Barumma, but he'd been away on business."

"So maybe Muka's bunch thought he'd be carrying a wad of money home?" Cord found Dimo's whisky bottle still intact, rose to his feet, poured two stiff measures into the plastic cups, and handed him one. "That might make sense."

"The diamond trade take few chances and Muka would know it. *Mungkin* . . . possibly ransom is a better bet, provided Chou Sie's family are the type who'd want him back." Dimo took a long, thankful swallow from the cup then hauled the smashed remains of his spectacles from one pocket and twirled them between long fingers. "Well, these are finished — but there should still be a spare pair in my suitcase, praise Allah!"

Cord chuckled. It seemed difficult to imagine anything the suitcase couldn't produce. "Praise Allah, like you said."

Slightly sheepishly, Dimo nodded and swirled the whisky in his cup. "You know, I am a Muslim — well, the fringe variety. We're a long way from Mecca. But just this once I can justify touching spirits." He found his handkerchief, soaked it in what was left of the liquor, and dabbed the moist cloth against his forehead. It stung against the cut and he grimaced. "*Hai* . . . that hurts. But at least it shouldn't leave a scar like — like . . . " he stopped unhappily.

"Like this?" Unperturbed, Talos Cord flicked a finger against the thin crescent-line on his left cheek. "No, it won't. But I've lived with mine a long time. I'd almost miss it."

Dimo frowned, his usual brashness absent. "I didn't mean . . . "

"Forget it." Beneath their feet, the deck began to tremble. The *Tari* was getting under way again. "Tell me about this thug Muka. He's got a reputation?"

"Uh-huh." Dimo nodded vigorously. "When an *orang-laut* crew turn pirate they join a kind of fraternity — like lodge-brothers. But not Muka and his men. For a start, *muka* simply means 'face' and nobody except maybe his crew has ever seen what he looks like. The other pirate outfits don't know a thing about them or where they come

61

from — the boat just appears, pulls a raid, usually something big, then vanishes again, sometimes for months."

He hunkered down and began exploring the suitcase. At first count, he'd lost a tin of cigarettes and a small travelling alarm. Cord left him to check the rest and went along to Kate Shellon's cabin.

It had been tidied back to normal when he arrived, but the story was the same — a rough search, a few minor items looted. Up on the top bunk, Sadiah Beh frowned in concentration over their precious recording equipment, checking item by item. He left them and walked slowly along the deck towards his own bunk.

The *Tari* was plodding on through peaceful seas, her pistons thudding the same asthmatic rhythm. The whole episode might never have happened, except for the scatter of bullet holes high on the coaster's upper works and the fact that her captain's cabin was once again free. Piracy might seem a wild anachronism back in twentieth-century Europe or America. But it still flourished in modern guise along the straggling sea-coasts from the Sulu Isles in the north right down to the Makasar Straits . . . and now he'd just been brushed by its surface.

In the cabin, Peter Dimo had already settled down for the night in the armchair. Yawning, Cord switched out the light, hung his jerkin behind the door, kicked off his moccasins, and decided that would be enough. He lowered himself on to the bunk's lumpy mattress and lay back.

A gentle snoring soon came from Dimo's corner and he pondered briefly over the young, strangely likeable Malaysian. For the moment, at least, he needed Peter Dimo and the gangling Rajah-Laut contact man was neither fool nor coward. That had been proved. But needing and trusting were two different things. More than once he'd had the impression Dimo was fencing with him — and in turn, Dimo had shown he had his own weakness.

Wriggling round, he sighed and cursed the bunk's discomfort. Still, he'd known worse. Almost without realising it, Cord let one hand stray again to the scar on his face. At least Dimo had tried to avoid being curious about it. Yet, in a way, the scar was part of what bound Talos Cord to Andrew Beck and Field Reconnaissance.

He'd been a scrawny eight year old when an Allied Officer — the same Andrew Beck — had found him in the post-Japanese surrender of a Shanghai internment camp. A large-eyed kid on his own, sheltered by an elderly White Russian ex-colonel and a faded Eurasian taxi-dancer from Bombay.

The scar had been a crusted wound when he'd been first delivered to the camp. Before that was a blank, no name, no past — only the fact that his ragged shirt had had 'P. Cord' handsewn into the neckband.

Beck had taken it from there, tracing back to a batch of civilians who'd tried to escape from Hong Kong. Their ship had been sunk, officially with no survivors. But now there was Peter Cord, no known kin — only Andrew Beck with his deep, soft, growling voice.

How much was affection, how much long-term vision in what followed? Cord still couldn't be sure. But Beck had re-christened him Talos, civilised him to things like wearing shoes and learning table manners — and each night that quiet, low-pitched voice had retold the story of the ancient Cretan myth behind his new name.

The first Talos had belonged to King Minos of Crete — a giant bronze robot built by the same Daedalus who sought to fly with feather wings. Faithful and incorruptible, untiringly constant, the robot Talos had enforced the rule of law throughout the island kingdom. Invaders felt its fire-breathing wrath, including a Mediterranean wanderer called Jason, who claimed he was searching for a Golden Fleece.

Only now, looking back, could Cord realise how right from the start, by environment, example and constant training, Andrew Beck had set out to mould his own Talos, one conditioned to regard the ideals behind the lumbering machinery of the brand new United Nations as his personal creed.

In the darkness, Cord grinned. The first Talos had broken down when a woman named Medea had pulled a drainplug loose and the robot's magic fluid had escaped. That was a fate he'd decided to avoid by a close study of the potential enemy. Andrew Beck didn't approve. But even Beck had to realise that his Talos was no metal machine.

Something small and needle-like stabbed briefly at his right leg and he slapped it wearily. Usually, when he was on a job, there was a U.N. agency of some kind within calling distance, a link which reduced the basic loneliness. This time he was on his own — well, maybe not completely. There was Dimo's slightly suspect company. And he wasn't forgetting Kate Shellon. Not by any means.

Something else bit, this time at knee level. Sleepily, he cursed the *Tari*'s first mate and rolled over.

* * *

It was mid-morning when the coaster reached Barumma, threading in through a scatter of mudbanks and fishing canoes. On deck, Cord saw little to rouse enthusiasm. The town — if it justified that title — sat in a cleared area which appeared in imminent danger of being swallowed up again by the flat, green jungle beyond. A river flowed in at the north end, and the water being churned by the *Tari*'s propeller was a rich, unhealthy yellowish brown.

"The River Ular," said Kate Shellon, leaning beside him at the rail. "Over there . . ." she pointed south, to what looked like a continuation of the mainland, but with the jungle reduced to rough, patchy scrub " . . . that bit's actually two small islands, Kuwa and Lapay. Lapay's where Sadiah and I should get some really good recordings within the next few days. You can drive from the mainland out to both, by causeway."

"Who gave you the geography lesson — Sadiah?" queried Cord.

"No, I bought a map back in Manilla and swotted up," confessed the redhead. "Sadiah's as much in the dark as I am about what's ashore. But we're being met."

"By this Tan Sallong study group?" They were coming in towards a long, wooden pier, the lower timbers spongy with marine growth. And so far the only reception committee he could see on the pier consisted of drab army uniforms and leather holsters.

"That's the arrangement." It took no great perception to see she was excited about the programme ahead. "Looks like time I went and made sure we're packed. I — I suppose we'll see you around?"

Cord grinned and nodded towards the town. "From the size of the place I'd say it was inevitable."

"Good." She smiled, then headed away.

In no hurry, he lounged back against the superstructure, the sunbaked metal warm against his back. On the pier, someone had already spotted the bullet holes on the *Tari*'s upper works and hands were pointing.

They moored and, once the gangway was secured, the first of the reception committee came trooping aboard — two army officers in drab green uniforms, one with a briefcase tucked under his left arm. At the shore end of the gangway, a soldier had taken up post with rifle and bayonet. Obviously nobody, but nobody, landed at Barumma until formalities were completed.

Almost a quarter hour passed before Peter Dimo came looking for him.

"All fixed." Dimo's spare spectacles

were identical to the ones he'd lost. He'd sponged the bloodstains from his suit and a strip of white adhesive plaster from the magic suitcase covered the cut on his forehead. "We're going ashore with Major Karog, next stop Colonel Suramo." He gave a slight, cautionary grin. "Karog is number two man around here, so don't let him rile you."

He followed Dimo back to the cabin. The officer with the briefcase was waiting outside, smoking a cigarette in a short, tortoiseshell holder. Major Karog was slim and immaculate, with hard, intelligent eyes in a strong Mongolian face, and when he switched on a five second smile he showed teeth almost too white and perfect.

"Mr Cord?" Karog gave a vague, perfunctory salute which stopped several inches short of his peaked army cap. "You still have your passport after last night's — ah — affair?"

Cord nodded and handed it over. Karog flicked through the passport's pages with minimum interest then returned it.

"We have, of course, already begun a search for these criminals." Karog's voice held the clipped intonation standard to accustomed authority. "Indonesia will not tolerate such outrages. You lost papers of importance in this wallet?"

"No, just some of my travelling money and a few bits and pieces." Cord raised a questioning eyebrow. "I thought they knocked out the radio?"

"It was sufficiently repaired to signal us this morning." Karog showed a slight impatience. "And your luggage? It will save delay . . ."

"Help yourself." Cord led the way into the cabin. Once again, Karog's attitude was one of apparent disinterest. He prodded the opened travel bag with a vaguely distasteful fore-finger, then tapped one of the film boxes.

"These?"

"Unexposed film."

"Open one, please. This one."

Cord stripped the sealing tape and

opened the lid. Major Karog glanced at the tightly packed cassettes, then lifted out one of the little white metal containers and hefted it thoughtfully. "You have a surprising number of these."

"I plan to take a lot of photographs." Cord met his gaze calmly.

"*Baik* . . . " Karog replaced the cassette and gestured him to repack the box. He smoked gently on his cigarette, then, as Cord finished and zipped the bag shut, moved towards the door. "I have a car waiting, if you are both ready."

Two cars were parked at the shore end of the pier. A young Indonesian in shirt and shorts, a white Panama hat perched on his head, was loading luggage into the trunk of a late model black Packard. The other, an olive green station wagon, had its engine ticking over and an army corporal in the driving seat. Cord glanced back towards the *Tari*. Kate Shellon and Sadiah were just leaving the coaster, one on either side of an elderly, shirt-sleeved European.

"Please." Major Karog gestured towards the station wagon, then, as Cord followed Dimo into the rear seat, closed the door behind them and took his place beside the driver.

"Headquarters," snapped Karog. As the station wagon began moving, he swung round. "You will understand, Mr Cord, that you can take no photographs, that you are not even officially ashore until a permit has been issued. But — ah — if the district governor agrees you will, of course, receive co-operation."

"Jameson Taggart at Tawau has sent an introduction . . ." began Dimo, leaning forward.

"You told me." Karog gave a bleak smile. "This, of course, is not Tawau. And Mr Cord will appreciate our need for control of certain activities as — as a matter of public safety."

"I appreciate," nodded Cord dryly as the vehicle's springs jolted them over a pothole. "Major, what's the chances for the man they grabbed last night?"

"The diamond merchant? If it is ransom, his family should hear soon enough." Karog shrugged with scant concern and faced his front, apparently uninterested in further conversation.

Cord gave up. They were travelling along a dusty, concrete strip lined on either side by an unimpressive straggle of two-storey structures and open-fronted shops. The people around moved unhurriedly, black Muslim caps bobbing amid turban headgear), the women, young and old, mostly in long, colourful wrapround cotton skirts with loose overblouses. Other road traffic was restricted to a few market trucks and a swarm of bicycles. He winced as a lean, hungry-looking dog avoided their front wheels by inches. But their corporal driver steered with a complete indifference to obstacles on two feet or four.

Further on, as the road changed from concrete to tar-sealed dirt, the

74

surroundings thinned to a scatter of thatched huts and carefully tilled vegetable patches which in turn gave way to a stretch of tall green casuarina pines. Then, suddenly, they were in a wide clearing edged by a high barbed-wire fence, a large house dominating its centre.

The station wagon swung off towards an open gate where a uniformed sentry, rifle slung, stood beside a small brick guard-post. They drove through without slowing and bounced on up a driveway leading to the sprawling house ahead. It was single-storey Dutch colonial style, with a stretch of grass lawn around it and, to one side, the red and white Indonesian flag hung limp from a high flagpole in the windless air.

A soldier hurried from the house to open the doors as the vehicle halted. They left their luggage and followed Major Karog into the building, past another armed sentry. Inside, the hallway was cool and high ceilinged, the walls panelled in wood, a few brass plaques the only decoration.

"If you will wait in here . . . " Karog waved them into a small, barely furnished room with a window which looked out towards the flagpole then left them, closing the door firmly behind him.

"A competent man, Major Karog," Peter Dimo spoke loudly, winked heavily, and continued talking as he walked across the room. "And when you meet Colonel Suramo you'll see that I was right — it takes a strong man to run a district like Barumma so smoothly." He stopped beside a heavily carved bureau, grinned as he put a finger to his lips, then stooped and pointed to its underside.

Cord tiptoed over, bent down, and saw the thin wire hidden beneath. One end vanished into the wall, the other terminated in a coin-sized microphone. He nodded and moved back as softly as he'd come. Then, noisily, he cleared his throat.

"Think there'll be any problem about

this permit, Peter?" He winked in turn. "You know, this picture series will make a lot of coverage, and I'd say what I want is right here. I like the angle of building up the story round the district governor, as a man with a load of responsibilities."

"Colonel Suramo would be a good subject," agreed Dimo quickly, taking his cue for their listener's benefit.

"Of course, I suppose they could say 'no'." Cord made a quick, rude gesture towards the hidden microphone. "Then I'd just have to try one of the other districts. I could always tell head office things weren't what we expected in this part — after last night's business that would be easy enough to explain."

"But unfortunate," said Dimo solemnly. "Very unfortunate." Cord moved over to the window. Outside, beyond the flagpole, two more armed guards were making a patrol round the length of the wire fence. Colonel Suramo was obviously a man who took few chances.

They waited quietly in the room for a few minutes more then the door opened and an orderly entered. The man signalled them to follow and led the way down the hallway to another doorway. He knocked, there was an answering growl from inside, and the orderly ushered them in.

The room was long and broad, with wide French doors opening out on to a verandah at the far end. A vast mahogany desk acted as its focus point, strategically placed so that the natural light came from behind its user. Not that the man behind the desk appeared to need any psychological gimmicks. Like a large, fleshy, frowning bear, a bear with a short waxed moustache and the last remaining strands of hair carefully greased across his scalp, Colonel Kaan Suramo sat in his shirt sleeves, with the top three collar buttons open to show a glistening expanse of flabby chest. Major Karog stood beside him at the desk. A few feet away, an Indonesian in a light grey lounge suit lounged comfortably in a leather armchair.

"Ah!" Karog stiffened as if on parade. "Colonel, may I present . . . "

"I know." Colonel Suramo's voice was a slightly weary rumble. "Mr Cord, *salam* . . . and welcome to Barumma And you, Dimo."

"It's good to see you again, Colonel," declared Dimo as they came forward.

"Not many say that and fewer mean it." The district governor's small dark eyes raked them suspiciously. Then he waved a thick paw towards the stranger. "Another visitor, one who wanted to meet you. Doorn Allat is a diamond buyer — he knew the man these damned *pembunuh* thugs seized last night."

"*Salam*, Mr Cord." Doorn Allat rose to his feet, his sallow, high-cheeked face serious but apparently friendly. He was burly without being fat and his handshake was a purely token pressure. "Chou Sie is a man I know only slightly, but many of my colleagues are

79

his old friends. *Menakutkan* . . . what has happened is horrifying. They will be anxious for news."

"There's not much we can tell you," Cord told him bluntly. "We didn't even know he was aboard till it happened."

"Even so, you can tell your friends that our visitors showed a certain restraint when he struggled," murmured Peter Dimo. "That is a good sign. And perhaps the *Tari*'s captain knows more . . ."

Major Karog shook his head firmly. "All he says is that Chou Sie arranged to have the cabin, then came aboard an hour before sailing and stayed in the cabin from then on. He swears no one was told of the arrangement, but *orang-laut* find out most things."

"You think Chou Sie guessed there might be trouble?" queried Dimo.

"In our business, Mr Dimo, there is always risk," said Allat non-committally.

Cord nodded. There was something nudging his memory, nudging yet failing to connect. "You mentioned colleagues, Mr Allat. You mean other diamond people?"

Allat nodded. "From all over — I myself am from Sumatra." One hand waved briefly and expressively. "The diamond diggings on Kuwa Island are Government owned and only once every year there is an official auction of stones. The next is in a few days' time — and so we are here to bid."

"It could make good picture material," suggested Dimo quickly. "That's the kind of thing you're looking for, Talos."

Cord heard Colonel Suramo rumble under his breath and, for his own part, silently cursed the young Malaysian. He nodded, but switched away from delicate ground. "It might. For now — well, Mr Allat, maybe Chou Sie will still make it."

"As long as he is safe. That is what matters. Later of course, if I can help you it will be a pleasure, Mr Cord." He bowed slightly towards Suramo. "You have work to do here, so I will leave you. *Selamat pagi . . .* "

"*Selamat.*" Colonel Suramo growled the goodbye and scratched pensively at his brown expanse of chest while Major Karog showed the diamond buyer out of the room. When he returned, Karog grudgingly dragged forward a couple of chairs.

"Sit down, gentlemen." Colonel Suramo watched them settle through half-closed eyes. "Now, Mr Cord, you have a letter from my good friend Taggart?"

"That's right." Cord handed it over. Suramo read the letter, his face expressionless, then passed it on to Karog without comment. Major Karog gave it the same treatment then carefully laid the sheet on the desk just out of Cord's reach. At last, Suramo broke the silence.

"You want to take pictures, Mr Cord — but what kind of pictures?" His left hand came down flat on the desk and stayed there, fingers tapping slowly. A thick gold ring on the little finger had a large diamond set in its centre. "Like some other parts of Indonesia, we have our troubles and difficulties — the kind Europeans like to hear about so that they can sit back and sneer at those foolish, ignorant natives they used to rule. As a result, we are careful, very careful. You should not be here. People like yourself make application to Central Government."

"But in Barumma you're district governor," said Cord easily. "And according to Peter Dimo, you decide most things."

"Hmm." Suramo glanced sharply in Dimo's direction, but the young Malaysian was carefully looking away, towards the French windows. His hand left the desk and stroked lightly along his waxed moustache. "What would you say, Karog?"

Major Karog frowned. "Like you, sir, I want to know what kind of photographs Mr Cord would take."

"A mixture — human interest, new methods of industry and agriculture, social development. All the ways in which Barumma is advancing." Cord played his trump with delicate care. "Naturally, I'd want your advice on subject matter — and your own responsibilities as district governor would have to be featured. I'd hope for a picture session with you during the time."

"I see." The broad face showed a thawing interest. Suramo slowly opened a finely carved wooden box, took out a cigarette, and lit it with a match he struck between finger and thumb. "How long would all this take?"

"About a week. The exact length would depend on — well, the degree of co-operation."

Suramo grunted and drew hard on the cigarette while his eyes showed a strange flicker of satisfaction. "*Baik* .... it might be arranged. But there would be firm conditions. Major Karog is responsible for security. I might have him place a vehicle and — ah — a guide at your disposal. The guide would have instructions. Let us say he would be advised where you should go."

"And where I shouldn't?" Cord grimaced cheerfully. "It's your district, Colonel. I'd say we could work things out."

"Good." Suramo scratched again at his chest. "Then you can take your pictures as from tomorrow. There is only one difficulty remaining." His mouth tightened, as if what he had to say left a bitter taste. "The diamond diggings on Kuwa are not, unfortunately, under my control. My colleague, Colonel Pappang, has that responsibility and can be regrettably unco-operative. I will tell him of your purpose, but you must make your own approach."

Cord nodded. "I'll do that. Anything more?"

"No. Later Major Karog will advise you of arrangements." Abruptly, Suramo switched his attention to Peter Dimo. "Now, I hear that Rajah-Laut also has problems . . . "

"But they're slightly involved," said Dimo lazily. He put a hand into his inside pocket, drew out a sealed, bulky envelope, and placed it in front of the man. "I've — ah — sketched out our situation. I'd like to talk it over once you've had a chance to examine the details."

"This afternoon, then. About four o'clock." Carefully ignoring the envelope, Suramo hauled himself to his feet. "Mr Cord, I have a thought. Tomorrow evening I am giving a small party — your friends from the *Tari*, Miss Shellon and Miss Beh, will be there. They are interested in our past, you in our future — my interests lie with both. Perhaps you and Dimo could join us."

They thanked him and the interview was over. Major Karog escorted them out of the room and along the hallway, then came to a halt as they reached the main door.

"The driver will take you to your hotel," said Karog stiffly. "I wish you a pleasant stay, Mr Cord."

"Things seem to have started well, anyway," grinned Cord. "Thanks, Major."

Karog's hard, dark eyes held cold disinterest. "Your thanks are due to the colonel, Mr Cord — and perhaps to Rajah-Laut. But not to me." He inclined his head in a fractional bow. "*Sekarang* . . . I will contact you later."

"Friendly," said Cord mildly, watching the soldier march back down the long corridor.

Peter Dimo chuckled, one hand combing through his thick, black hair. "Maybe he guessed what was in that envelope. I've heard that the major doesn't always approve of his boss's devotion to profit."

"You mean . . ."

"Uh-huh. Our quarterly retainer. Captain Muka and his mob aren't the only pirates around here." Dimo gestured towards the waiting station wagon. "Now I want a shower and a long, cold beer. Then food. Sound okay?"

Cord stayed where he was for a moment, not answering. Karog's attitude was one thing. But somehow, by instinct, hunch, anything else an outsider might have called it, he had a sudden doubt about the way things had gone in Suramo's office. It was almost as if he'd been inspected, chosen for a purpose, then gently manœuvred into the first stage of a complex web. If he was right — well, it might have some strange advantages.

"Hey . . . " Dimo was standing by the door, waiting.

"I'm coming." Slowly, pensively, Cord walked towards him.

3

ON the south side of town, the Harimau Hotel was a drab, four-storey brickwork box with the sign of a thin, dyspeptic tiger over its entrance. Talos Cord eyed the painting bleakly, hoping it hadn't been intended as an artist's sour-humoured warning.

"I usually take a room here," said Peter Dimo, as the station wagon drove off, leaving them standing at the Harimau's entrance. "There's another place, but they don't change the bedding so often."

"You're the expert," reminded Cord. "I'm just tourist material." He followed Dimo in through the wide swing doors into a reception area which was shabby but cool and reasonably clean. A gloomy Indian desk clerk watched them sign the register.

"Look . . . " Dimo pointed to the book and gave a happy murmur. A few lines above their newly penned signatures were two familiar enough names — Kate Shellon and the Indonesian girl were once again their neighbours. Casually, Cord glanced over the other entries and flicked back a page. Most of the current guests at the Harimau seemed to have arrived within the last forty-eight hours. He remembered the diamond buyers, smiled a little at the wealthy company he was keeping, but couldn't find Doorn Allat's name among the list.

"*Tuan* . . . " an elderly porter, stoop-shouldered, with bad breath, sucked his teeth politely. Cord closed the book and went with him to where Dimo was already waiting in a tiny, box-like elevator. It creaked up to the top floor and they were shown their rooms, side by side at the far end of the corridor, simply furnished, a narrow, cupboard-like washroom with shower leading off each.

"*Terima!*" Dimo tipped the porter and, as the man shuffled off, gave a contented sigh. "About that beer, Mr. Cord — should we say downstairs, in half an hour?"

"I'll be there, ready and thirsty," promised Cord. He went back into his room, closed the door, and waited. Soon, through the thin partition wall, he could hear water running and the occupant singing in an off-key tenor. He grinned, opened the travel bag, and took out the film boxes, emptying their neatly stocked cassettes on the bed. Two larger tins, flat and oblong, fell out in the process. Each was marked 'Exposed Film — Open in Darkroom.' Cheerfully, he ripped off the sealing tape.

The first tin held a Swiss Neuhausen automatic wrapped in an oily rag. The other had half a dozen clips of fat, glistening 9 mm Parabellum cartridges packed tight within. Field Reconnaissance preferred brain to brawn or bloodshed. But when the options ran

91

out, even a peacemaker had a right to bear arms.

Cord looked around the room and found what he wanted inside the dressing table, a shallow, hidden space above the top drawer. There was a roll of adhesive tape in the travel bag and, in a couple of minutes, automatic and ammunition were strapped firmly in place above the drawer-space. Satisfied, he slid the drawer back into position and reckoned it would take a particularly skilful or lucky searcher to locate them.

The job done, he could afford to relax. The film cassettes back in their boxes, the rest of his bag unpacked, he walked into the bathroom, stripped off his clothes, and forgot everything for the next couple of minutes while the stinging bliss of the cold-water shower played hard on his naked body. When he'd finished, a threadbare towel was waiting on a nail beside the tap. He rubbed himself down, pulled on shirt and slacks, and padded barefoot back into the room. Then he stopped short, poised on the balls of his feet, his eyes on the unexpected visitor who sat over by the window in the room's only chair.

It took a moment to recognise the captain of the *Tari*. The Indonesian wore a business suit of cotton duck, balanced a battered soft hat on his knees, and gave a rather uneasy smile of greeting.

"*Tuan* Cord . . ."

"What the hell do you want?" Cord crossed towards him, frowning but relieved. "I prefer people to knock . . ." a wisp of humour crossed his mind as he remembered when he'd last heard the same sentiments. "Well?"

"*Tuan*, I came here quietly and, *Masja Allah*, I would leave the same way." The man's voice stayed low, his English slow and painful. "Even being here I run a risk." He looked at Cord hopefully. "And, of course, I have no thought of reward."

"Good — I'd no particular thought

of paying one." Cord perched himself on the edge of the bed, disliking the fat, sweating face opposite yet seeing the nervous fear in the man's eyes. "Not in advance anyway."

The sailor swallowed and licked his lips. "Last night, when the accursed *orang-laut* boarded us, their hell-born Captain Muka took me from the rest and asked many questions about you. When he finished he warned me to say nothing, that they might yet have business with you."

"What kind of questions?" Cord stirred, interested.

"Who you were, when you booked passage, who you had spoken to aboard . . ." the man shrugged. "With a gun in my stomach, I did as any wise man would and told them what I knew. There is more." He stopped and looked uneasily around the room, as if expecting to see Muka's raiders emerge from the walls. "But as I said, there is risk to me in it."

"Then don't force yourself." Cord

let one hand stray to his hip pocket and brought out a fold of rupiah notes. Slowly, he began to count them through. "What's your name?"

"Chealu — Captain Chealu." The eyes were on the notes. Cord let five flutter down one by one on the bed. Each was for a hundred rupiahs. "*Tuan*, since we docked other men have asked questions about you."

"Major Karog's soldiers?"

A quiver crossed the fat, sweating face but Chealu shook his head. "Other men, strangers — two of them, and not Borneo men by their tongues."

"They spoke to you?"

"*Aduh* . . . yes, with a gun again in my stomach and a warning to stay silent. But I have come." He glanced from Cord to the notes and back again. "It seemed right you should be warned."

"You'd know them again?"

Reluctantly, the sailor nodded. "One at least, a barrel-like man with a withered left arm. He — he said

95

something I cannot understand. It was that if you are a photographer like I told him there will soon be pictures to be taken in plenty. But if you are not, you will soon have something much heavier than a camera round your neck."

Cord could imagine the alternatives available. "That's all he said?"

"Just that, and then he laughed." Captain Chealu reached out, his fingers brushing lightly over the rupiah notes. Cord nodded, and the money was scooped up in a single motion. The sailor rose to his feet. "*Tuan*, the *Tari* does not sail again until tomorrow night. If you are interested, there is at least one place aboard where even Captain Muka's men would not find you . . ."

"Thanks for the offer," said Cord dryly. "I'll let you know." He saw the man out, closed the door, then gave a wry wink at his own reflection in the crackled glass of the dressing table mirror. One way and another he was being drawn into things without having to try particularly hard.

The room window faced the front of the hotel. He crossed over, looked down, and waited. In a few moments Captain Chealu left the building by the main door. The sailor stopped for a moment, glanced anxiously around, then set off at a rapid pace towards the harbour. Cord waited long enough to be sure no one was apparently following the man, then he turned away and finished dressing.

★ ★ ★

The Harimau's bar was on the ground floor, and quiet. Two Dutchmen, planters by their appearance, were drinking at a corner table. At the far end of the counter, a lone Indonesian hunched sleepily over a thimble glass of rice wine. Talos Cord paid for a lager and took his change in a handful of strong black Dusun cheroots. When Peter Dimo appeared, he was already halfway through the first cheroot and toying with the last of the beer in his glass.

"I'll catch up." Dimo beckoned, and the bartender filled another glass. Like Cord's drink, the beer was lukewarm but foam-topped. Dimo took a long, happy swallow then wiped his lips. "Sending a cable out of here is hard work — but Rajah-Laut's golden rule is 'keep in touch.'"

Cord chewed the cheroot stub gently between his teeth. "I'm supposed to do the same. What's the drill?"

"For a cable? Just hand it to the desk clerk." Dimo's voice dropped a fraction. "But keep it simple. Suramo will get a copy."

They finished the drinks and moved through to the dining room. Soup was followed by a cake-like mixture of rice, vegetables and finely chopped fish. It tasted better than it looked and by the time the shirt-sleeved waiter brought coffee in small, handleless cups Cord felt all was much better with the world.

He found Dimo looking at him in quizzical fashion.

"Something wrong?"

The young Malaysian shook his head. "I get curious about people, that's all." Abruptly, he pushed his cup aside. "I won't be around this afternoon. Any plans?"

"Look the town over, I think. That's about all."

"You'll have company," Dimo told him easily. "The table near the door."

Cord glanced briefly. The Indonesian who'd been in the bar was eating on his own. "You mean the colonel's allocated me a personal watchdog?"

"First-timers here usually rate one," agreed Dimo. "But he's a Karog man, not Suramo's."

"There's a difference?"

"A big difference, according to Major Karog." Dimo got to his feet. "See you later, okay?"

Cord nodded. Once Dimo had gone he asked the waiter to bring him a pencil and paper then scribbled out

99

the cablegram. It was a short, plain-language message that he'd reached Barumma and was addressed to the Paris head-quarters of the magazine group — which was genuine enough. But the Indonesian cable link to Europe still ran through Singapore, and Field Reconnaissance would collect it from there.

He lingered over the coffee a little longer then at last left the dining room, spoke to the Indian desk clerk, and arranged for the cable to be despatched. Another of the cheroots glowing between his lips, he strolled out of the building, conscious that Karog's watchdog was once again not far behind.

It took about an hour's apparently aimless wandering around the squalid, fly-plagued little town before he could be sure he had a reasonable idea of its layout. The basic land-marks were the Harimau Hotel, the harbour, and the high minaret tower of a white-washed mosque. The rest was noise and bustle, radios blaring from open shops, half-naked children shouting as they raced up and down narrow alleyways and plagued scarecrow-like beggars, the occasional vehicle rumbling past the rest of the pedal-powered traffic.

The watchdog was still there, thin and tireless, keeping about thirty yards behind. Gradually, Cord retraced his steps until he was almost back at the hotel, in a quiet sidestreet. A lane, deserted and empty, ran off it between two warehouses. Cord swung into it smartly, saw a doorway just ahead, and glanced back. The mouth of the lane was still empty. He moved into the doorway, pressed himself back, and waited.

In a moment, he heard swift footsteps. Karog's man had reached the lane, saw it was empty, and was worried. As he hurried past, eyes fixed ahead, Cord stepped out behind him, right arm sweeping down in a long, chopping stroke. The edge of his hand caught the watchdog hard on the back of the neck — and Cord caught him as he fell, dragging him back into the doorway.

"Now then . . . " he grinned almost apologetically at the unconscious form propped against the wall " . . . let's give both of us an alibi."

There was a heavy automatic in a holster under the man's left arm. He took the gun, searched through the jacket's pockets, and collected a thin billfold and a plastic covered warrant card identifying the man as a military police sergeant. As a final touch, he stripped off the watch on one wrist, arranged the man into a pose as if sleeping, then left the lane and headed back towards the busier section of town.

Halfway along, he got rid of the gun and watch in one of the open, garbage-filled ditches which seemed Barumma's main drainage system. The wallet and warrant card in his hip pocket, he kept on until he spotted a silversmith's shop, went in through the narrow doorway, and looked round the gloomy interior.

"*Tuan?*" The silversmith, an old man with a beard dyed bright henna red, broke off tapping out the shape of a brooch on a small anvil and regarded him hopefully.

"*Tolong* . . . " Cord greeted him politely. "I seek the home of the diamond merchant Chou Sie."

With a sigh, the silversmith gave up thoughts of a sale and nodded. The directions were reasonably straightforward. The diamond merchant's house was on the edge of town, near the river. Cord thanked the man, took out the sergeant's bill-fold, and extracted a fifty rupiah note. The henna beard broke in a brief smile of thanks.

Another five minutes walking took him to the place. Houses nearest the River Ular obviously belonged to the wealthier section of Barumma's community, some with small walled gardens, a few hardly distinguishable from European bungalows. Chou Sie's was an airy, single-storey structure with a pagoda-like roof of red tiles. A jeep stood outside, empty, and Cord came to a sudden halt as he saw two people together on the house porch.

Even at that distance there was no difficulty in recognising Peter Dimo. Eyes narrowed, Cord retreated a few paces to where a thick rhododendron bush grew man-high by the road-side, fat bees humming around a luxuriant pink flourish of blossom. From its shelter, he watched. The other figure on the porch was a small, middle-aged woman and whatever the conversation she'd been having with the young Malaysian it appeared just about over. He saw Dimo reach out and lay a hand on the woman's shoulder, speaking earnestly. The woman gave a slow, unhappy nod then, as Dimo turned and walked back towards the jeep, she went slowly into the house, her shoulders bowed, her manner weary.

The jeep's engine fired. Cord edged further into the shelter of the rhododendron as the little vehicle swung round on the road and a moment later it came past him, gears changing noisily, tyres stirring up the dust. Behind the wheel, eyes fixed ahead, Peter Dimo's boyish features were somehow harder and older, the mouth tight and angry.

A bee buzzed a lazy, pollen-laden path towards Cord's head. He brushed it aside and, as the jeep disappeared round a bend in the road, started to leave cover. Then, suddenly, another engine started up, revving hard, and he froze instinctively as a high-sprung grey sedan came bouncing out from behind a patch of thick scrub some three hundred yards beyond the house. The car reached the road and swung towards him, gathering speed. Once more he side-stepped into the screen of blooms and this time, as the car went past, he whistled softly as the sight of its occupant.

Hands clenched tight on the steering wheel, Doorn Allat's sallow face was a carved mask of unemotional purpose. The diamond merchant was in his shirt sleeves and the strap of what might have been binoculars was slung round his neck. Another cloud of dust billowed like an obscuring fog from the sedan's tyres, and as it settled the car was already swinging round the bend in the road, following the wake of Dimo's jeep.

That part was the young Malaysian's worry. Pensively, Talos Cord considered the pagoda-roofed house. There might be another watcher around, but somehow he doubted it, Mind made up, he strode forward, reached a raked gravel path, and crunched his way up to the front door. A heavy brass knocker was set at eye-level. He rapped twice, waited, heard slow footsteps, and the door swung open.

The woman he'd seen earlier peered out at him silently from the gloom of the hallway. She was older than he'd realised, her complexion like wrinkled parchment, her sunken eyes holding a strained hostility at this latest intrusion on her grief.

"*Salam* . . . you are the wife of Chou Sie?" Cord spoke slowly and gravely in his best Indonesian, saw her fractional nod, and went on. "My name is Cord and I was on the *Tari* last night."

"*Mari masuk*." Her voice resigned, she opened the door a few inches wider, allowed him in, then led the way into a small front room where an old-fashioned upright piano reigned amid a scatter of low chairs. A faint scent of incense was in the air, and one corner held a small Chinese-style family altar, framed by ancestral pictures. She sat down, waited until he'd followed her example, then asked, "Why have you come, *Tuan* Cord?"

"To ask if I could help, or if there was news . . ."

She shook her head. "There is nothing. You knew my husband?"

"No, but I saw what happened," said Cord, hating himself a little for what he was doing. "And I have met his friends — one of them another *berlian*

107

merchant, a man called Doorn Allat. You know him?"

She frowned. "*Tidak* . . . no, but I have heard that name."

"He is from Sumatra," prompted Cord.

"Ah." She nodded her understanding. "My husband goes there sometimes to trade in stones." The wrinkled face twitched briefly, then discipline took over again. "Another passenger from the ship is not long gone from here — a young man."

"Peter Dimo?" Cord nodded. "We travelled together. But I didn't know he was coming here."

"He also offered his help." She shrugged a little. "But who needs help to wait?" The thin fingers of one hand were rubbing against the arm of her chair in a way which told more of tension than any words. "My husband is an old man, Mr Cord, and he is also wealthy, though our needs are simple. But he is not a well man. If this Captain Muka wants ransom, my hope is he will not wait too long."

"And your husband has no enemies, none jealous of his business — or his politics?"

She was firmly positive in her answer. Chou Sie was a prudent man, with no interests beyond the diamond trade — and a man with no enemies as far as she was aware. And their friends were few, seldom visited.

At last, wearily, she finished and rose from her chair. "Now, *Tuan* Cord, I have thanked you for coming. But I am tired, I must rest."

He got to his feet. "Of course. But one thing still puzzles me. How would this Muka know your husband would be a passenger on the *Tari*?"

She shook her head. "*Entah*. . . . I do not know. He told no one when he left for the north. Even Colonel Suramo did not know and came to visit him on some matter." She pursed her lips in brief, bitter recollection. "I heard nothing of when he would be back until there was a *tilgram* from him yesterday morning."

Which meant just a few hours before the coaster had sailed from Tawau. Like the click of a rachet, it brought the possibilities a full cog forward. Cord frowned, considering the results. Suramo would have known of the cable. Suramo would have — he let the wild thought go on while he went through the motions of saying a polite goodbye and leaving. Yes, the colonel would have had the best part of a day in which to arrange for the pirate *kumpit* to intercept the coaster.

Outside, as the door closed behind him, the road seemed empty. If the house was still under observation any watchers were well hidden.

Which brought things back again to Doorn Allat. Had the diamond merchant — if he was one — been primarily interested in who came calling on Chou Sie's house or in Peter Dimo's movements? And either way, why?

Hands in his pockets, humming an old, half-forgotten snatch of tune, he started the walk in to Barumma. Coming out had been profitable, and now the harbour was next on his list. Someone down there had been asking questions about Talos Cord. Now, he wanted to ask a few of his own.

* * *

It was almost four p.m. by his wristwatch when he arrived at the harbour. The sun glared down from high in the west and, out in the same direction, the sea stretched in a vast, limpid blue. But the tide was out, which meant that the mud-flat debris of the harbour area was exposed in all its high-smelling decay, dark banks speckled with hundreds of noisy, white, feeding seabirds. Moorings high and dry, a scatter of dugout canoes and larger fishing boats lay stranded on their sides. Even the deep-water channel had shrunk to a narrow, dirty ribbon and alongside the pier the *Tari* showed an alarming amount of rust-red bottom plating.

111

Cord kept on, past a group of fishermen repairing their nets, threading between high-piled bales of copra and assorted labelled crates. The few dockers in sight worked at a slow, lethargic pace and in that kind of humidity he couldn't blame them. A medium-sized truck had been parked beside the *Tari*, canvas hood up and tailboard down, but it seemed deserted.

Another miniature mountain of baled copra loomed ahead. He stopped in its shade, mopped his brow with one sleeve, reached for a cheroot, then glanced round as he heard a soft chuckle of amusement.

"Finding it warm, Talos?" Kate Shellon came nearer, smiling, cool in a pale green cotton dress, her red hair like spun fire in the harsh sunlight, legs bare, her feet in sandals. "I'm about ready to melt."

"Let's say that if I was a steak I'd be in the medium-rare category." He glanced past her to where Sadiah Beh was approaching, an elderly European at her side — the man he'd seen with the girls earlier, as they left the *Tari*. "Found yourself a guide?"

"And a good one." She waited until they arrived. "Doctor Brink, this is the photographer I told you about." For Cord's benefit she added, "Doctor Brink is chairman of our sponsors here."

"Hendrik Brink — and as I prefer to make clear, I am not a medical man. My degree was in law, and now I am retired." The accent was heavily Dutch and the man was well in his sixties — small and sundried, with bright blue eyes, a slight limp as he walked, a white silk handkerchief protruding from the top pocket of his brown gaberdine jacket. "I'm sorry you had such an unpleasant introduction to our corner of the world, Mr Cord."

"I've filed it under 'local colour'. The rest seems seasonable." Cord turned his attention to Sadiah, who had a tan shirt-blouse tucked into dark, tailored slacks which were tight across the thighs. "Sight-seeing?"

"Getting our bearings," corrected the girl with a flash of white teeth. "We had just about decided it was time for a coffee break."

"And then Miss Beh spotted you," said Brink cheerfully. "You will join us, Mr Cord?"

"Well . . . " Cord hesitated, glanced briefly towards the *Tari*. Two men had appeared beside the truck's tailboard and were loading a packing case aboard, but the coaster was still otherwise deserted. "All right, thanks — I will."

"Good. It is not far." Smiling, the Dutchman led the way, limping a step or two ahead. Their destination was a small open-air waterfront café about a minute's walk distant and, as they took one of the marble-topped tables, Cord noted ruefully that the pier was no longer in view.

A waiter brought coffee on a tray. Kate Shellon reached for her cup, sipped, and sighed thankfully. "Now all I need is the chance to soak my feet somewhere."

"We have covered a good distance," admitted Brink. He beamed across at Cord. "But I chose this café for these young ladies for two particular reasons. Over there . . . " he pointed to his left, giving them time to turn " . . . Kuwa and Lapay, our magic islands. Kuwa, where the diamonds are, is the nearer, Mr Cord. But it is Lapay which matters most to us."

Magic islands they might be, but even from the new viewpoint of the café both Kuwa and Lapay appeared dull, unromantic stretches of scrub-covered rock and clay. Kuwa, the nearest, was separated from the mainland by a short stretch of tidal mud, spanned at one point by a broad, stone-built causeway. It might be a couple of miles long, but no more. Here and there a few low buildings were visible. More significantly, a barbed wire fence started just above the high-water mark, and what looked like a sandbagged machine-gun post was clearly visible at the far end of the causeway. Most of Lapay was hidden behind its neighbour, but what was visible held little promise.

"What's so special about Lapay?"

Kate Shellon and the Dutchman exchanged a glance of amusement but left it to Sadiah to answer.

"Because it is the Isle of Dragons! You mean you didn't know?" Her voice held an underlying scorn at such basic ignorance. "This is the time when the rice is planted after the monsoons — a time when the pagan peoples offered sacrifices for a safe crop. From all around here they came to the Isle of Dragons, danced, offered their gifts, then — then . . . "

"Then hoped for the best," completed Kate Shellon dryly. "The dragons were either sea snakes or king-sized monitor lizards. There are still some of both around Lapay. They rated as sacred."

"And the sacrifices?" Cord raised a wary eyebrow.

"Slaves who weren't fit enough to earn their keep. They staked them out on the beach."

"And saved on unemployment benefits?" Cord grimaced. He'd never come across a monitor lizard, but a shoal of sea snakes, thin, brown-backed, yellow-bellied whiplashes, constituted a nightmare by any standards. "What happens nowadays?"

Kate and Sadiah sat back, leaving that one to Doctor Brink. A large yellow and crimson butterfly fluttered down over the table and came to rest on the brown gaberdine of his jacket sleeve. Brink regarded it with tolerant disinterest.

"If you are here in two days' time you will see for yourself, Mr Cord," he promised. "One or two villages still pay lip-service to the old ways. Their people go out to Lapay, then spend the night carrying out the old rituals — except, of course, that the sacrifices are now merely symbolic." His mouth crinkled at the corners. "So far the

117

dragons haven't complained."

"And that's what I want to get, Talos," explained Kate Shellon, her freckled face suddenly earnest. "The Dragon Night songs and rituals on tape — it hasn't been done before. I thought I'd lost the chance until these permits came through."

Cord nodded. "Thanks to this Tan Sallong Society, right?" He glanced casually at the Dutchman. "It sounds like the local branch of Mafia International."

Doctor Brink frowned for a moment, then understood. "Ah — no, not quite." He tasted his coffee again, the movement sending the butterfly off on a fresh, fluttering search. "We are what you might call — let me see — yes, a cultural pressure group, both European and Indonesian."

"But Tan Sallong was a rebel . . ."

"A patriot before his time," corrected Brink with a touch of mock severity. "As the British also found out with their empire, yesterday's rebels are today's prime ministers. Tan Sallong's mistake was in being born too soon." He leaned forward, growing more earnest. "Mr Cord, I am old enough to face facts, unpalatable though they may have been when they occurred. Indonesia exists, but has still to become a nation. It is a collection of islands, most of them jungle — and of island peoples, with little trust for one another. Some are Stone-Age primitives, others are — ah — rather ingenious financial manipulators. In Borneo, we escaped the worst of the Communist rebellion and what we called the Stormking Executions when they were hunted down. But it showed what could happen unless people recognised their roots, knitted together . . . " he stopped, and blinked apologetically. "I'm sorry. I am beginning to make a speech."

"Colonel Suramo's one of your supporters, I know," murmured Cord. "What about the military boss out on Kuwa?"

"Colonel Pappang?" The Dutchman pursed his lips and shook his head.

"He is Javanese, an honest enough man, but unimaginative. He would stop the Dragon Night if he could — especially this year, when it comes on the same week as the diamond auctions are due."

"Why?" Cord showed his surprise. "Don't tell me the Dragon Dancers worry him?"

Brink shrugged. "There is another causeway linking Kuwa to Lapay — both were built by the Japanese during the war. Pappang refuses to let them be used, and the dancers must go to Lapay by boat. Still, perhaps he should not be blamed." His mouth tightened for a moment. "Two years ago there was another colonel on Kuwa who allowed the causeways to be used. The dancers were drunk on rice wine when they came back. They quarrelled with the Javanese soldiers — five soldiers were killed, at least eight of the dancers. Both sides remember."

Cord nodded his understanding.

"I'm hoping to contact Pappang and get the go-ahead to see over his island." The truck which had been loading at the pier was grinding along the road towards them and he watched it idly. "Most things around here seem run by the army, and tightly. Almost as if they were waiting for trouble. Are they?"

"Here?" Brink shook his head and turned reassuringly to the girls. "Like anywhere, there are problems — occasional piracy like your experience, a few bandits in the hills. But you will find people around Barumma are friendly, easy-going. Nature provides them enough to eat without undue effort, which is perhaps their problem in this century."

Kate Shellon said something in reply, but Cord was no longer listening. The truck was swaying past the café, two men in its open-sided cab. The driver was small and nondescript, but the Indonesian in the passenger seat was squat, built like a wrestler. He lolled back, a cigarette dangling between his

121

lips, talking to his companion. He wore a short-sleeved shirt, his left arm was nearest Cord — and that arm hung limp, withered, exactly as the *Tari*'s captain had described.

"Talos?" Kate Shellon's voice, faintly annoyed, forced him back to the table conversation.

"Sorry, I was day-dreaming." The truck had a sign on its side, proclaiming it the property of Tengah Imports. "Thinking about your Isle of Dragons," he added smoothly. "Must have been quite a place in the old days."

"And fascinating," chipped in Sadiah quickly. "The colours, the rhythms . . . "

"I was thinking of the characters they staked out." He received a faint sniff as his reward, but hardly noticed. The truck was turning off the road, swinging down a side-street about five hundred yards ahead. Wherever it was going, apparently it wasn't leaving town. Unhurriedly, he finished his coffee and glanced at his watch. "Well, thanks for your company. Kate, we're neighbours

122

again — I'm at the Harimau, with Peter Dimo."

"No room complications?" she asked, eyes twinkling.

"Not this time, but I'll come calling again."

"Naturally," murmured Doctor Brink. "But — you have to go, Mr Cord?"

"Still looking for pictures angles," he explained easily. "You never know what's available until you look."

He said goodbye, left them, and at first strolled off in the opposite direction from the way the truck had gone. But once out of sight he doubled back, using the rabbit-warren alleyways, skirting past the inevitable, high-smelling garbage piled outside almost every doorway. When he reached the side-street, the truck wasn't to be seen — but the street ran straight down towards the water. There was no way out for a vehicle. He walked on, moving slowly, every sense alert.

Halfway down, he heard voices and

a sudden, high-pitched laugh — then a wide entrance gate a little way ahead began to swing open. As it creaked, Cord made a dive for the shelter of the nearest alley and watched from the corner, pressed tight against the sunbaked brick wall.

Out of the gate came the two men from the truck, the smaller one still laughing. His companion thumped him on the back with his good arm and waited until the wooden gate had been swung shut again. The click of a padlock sounded loud, then both men moved off, heading down towards the shore but turning off into another alleyway after a few yards.

As they disappeared, Talos Cord drew a long, soft breath of relief. He stayed where he was a moment longer then crossed over to the gate. A sign to one side said it was the storage depot for Tengah Imports, and through a crack in the warped wood he could see into the walled yard on the other side, with the canvas roofed truck parked beside a long, tin-roofed warehouse shed. Nothing moved, the shed seemed locked and deserted.

Footsteps coming towards him brought his eyes round. He leaned back against the door pretending to light a cheroot while two dockers in ragged shorts and singlets shuffled by. They paid no attention to him. Once they'd gone, he sized up the gate. It was about seven feet high, but the padlock's massive hasp, set about halfway, could provide a toehold . . .

Muscles tensed, he flexed his body, jumped, got two firm handholds on the top spar, pulled, and at the same time got the edge of his right foot on the hasp. Next moment he was astride the gate. One last look around, and he dropped down in catlike style into the yard. Still nothing stirred. Quickly, he padded across the baked earth to the truck. The tailboard was in position, and the crate loaded from the *Tari* hadn't been removed.

He clambered in. It was cool and

dull under the canvas after the glaring sunlight, but he'd no time to appreciate the change. The crate was about twice the size of a tea chest, its lid nailed down. He swore softly, looked around, saw a tyre lever lying in one corner, and used it as a jemmy. Nails screeched briefly, then the lid had freed enough for him to finish the job by hand.

He didn't take the lid completely off. It wasn't necessary.

The coaster *Tari* was going to need a new master. Captain Chealu's body had been jammed inside the crate, knees against his chest. He was still wearing the same cotton duck suit, and the manner of his killing was plain. He head lolled at an obscene, unnatural angle.

Someone strong, very strong, had broken the sailor's neck. Cord thought of the man with the wrestler's build and one good arm. It would have been enough, properly used, aided by a knee in Chealu's back. And it would have been over in a couple of heartbeats.

He stood with the lid still half-raised for a moment longer, knowing there was nothing he could do — at least, not yet. Not until he knew a good deal more about how the cards were stacked. Then, mouth tight, the hairline scar a line of bitter anger, he let the wood down. A few light taps with the tyre lever and the nails were back in their holes.

Counting seconds now, he left the truck and checked the warehouse shed. It had one door, metal faced and double locked. The first window looked in on a small, untidy office. The others showed what looked like an endless succession of bales and crates, their markings impossible to read through the grimy glass.

There was no easy way in, and burglary in broad daylight would be a fool's move. But he could come back. He headed for the gate again.

★ ★ ★

Ten minutes later, hands in his pockets, a cheroot glowing between his lips, Talos Cord strolled into the Harimau Hotel with all the lazy ease of a man without cares. The Indian desk clerk saw him, stiffened, and cleared his throat noisily. Immediately, a thin, ill-tempered figure sprang up from a nearby chair.

"*Tuan* Cord . . . "

It was Major Karog's plain-clothes sergeant, his face tight and angry, his voice strained.

"Yes?" Cord smiled at him with bright unconcern.

"*Polisi*. Major Karog wishes to see you immediately, on official business."

"Does he, now?" Cord looked doubtful. "Let me see your warrant card. For all I know you could be one of that *peranpok* Muka's men."

"But it . . . " the man stopped and swallowed hard. "*Maafkan* . . . owing to circumstances I — I cannot do that. But the desk clerk knows me."

"Hold on." Cord swung round

towards the clerk, his whole manner radiating wary suspicion. "You know this man?"

"*Polisi*," confirmed the Indian anxiously. "He is *sergenti*, Mr Cord. You should go. Major Karog does not like to be kept waiting."

"All right. When my friend Dimo comes in, tell him what happened."

Uneasily conscious of the sergeant's wallet still resting snug in his jerkin's inside pocket, Cord gestured for the man to lead the way.

But whatever Karog wanted him for, this was no social invitation.

4

KAROG'S sergeant had a car parked a little way along the street. The man took care to see Cord aboard and the passenger door closed before he came round to his own side and, as he slid behind the wheel, a bulge under his jacket showed that at least one item of his equipment had been replaced.

The journey was brief, through the town and then up a small hill on its outskirts. The car halted at the door of a high-walled two-storey building which had a uniformed sentry outside and two radio masts towering from its roof.

Cord got out, then waited until the man joined him. There were iron bars on some of the building's windows, an official noticeboard beside the main door, and the other vehicles parked around were exclusively military, two of them armoured half-tracks.

"I thought Colonel Suramo's place was district headquarters," he said mildly.

The sergeant nodded. "*Ja*. But here is civil security, Major Karog's department."

They went in past the sentry, through an office where both uniformed and civilian personnel were at work and stopped at a door at the other end. The sergeant knocked, opened the door, looked in, then waved him to enter. "Ah, Mr Cord. You took a little finding." Karog rose lithely from behind his desk, showing his teeth in a fractional greeting. The room was small, furnished in spartan fashion, and the nearest thing to decoration was a weapon rack holding a 30-30 magnum rifle and a matched pair of pump-action shotguns with walnut stocks. As Cord took the chair opposite, Karog dismissed the sergeant with a nod. The man went out, closing the door.

"Well, Major?" Cord settled back, meeting the hard, bright eyes opposite. "I hope it's about tomorrow's details . . . "

"In part." Karog sat very still for a moment, arms folded. "As a matter of interest, where were you this afternoon?"

"Looking around town." Cord shrugged easily, deciding on half truths. "While I was at it, I took a trip out to that diamond buyer's home . . . "

"Chou Sie?" Karog didn't even try to look surprised. "Why?"

"Just in case his wife needed help — you know how it is. Then, well, I walked back into town, met the two girls who were with us on the *Tari*, and had coffee with them and a Doctor Brink. Seemed a pleasant old character."

"Quite. When the Dutch were here he was a magistrate." Karog's face relaxed a little. "I should warn you, Mr Cord, that it is not always safe for a European — a stranger — to wander through our backstreets. There have been — ah — one or two recent assaults on people in the less desirable sections. However, that is not why I asked you here." His right hand flicked aside one of the papers on his desk. "Do you recognise this?"

"Yes!" Cord stared down at the Swedish clasp-knife, with its multi-blades and bone handle. "It was . . . "

"In your luggage when the *Tari* was raided last night." A thin smile forced its way across Karog's sallow face. "And taken, as your friend Dimo reported. You identify it as your property?"

Cord nodded.

"*Baik*." Karog shoved the knife across the desk. "It is yours again. This morning, one of our patrols in the coastal jungle to the north had a brush with an armed group. One of the bandits was killed. They left various items behind which we know came from the *Tari*. This was in the man's pack."

"What about the rest of the bunch — and Chou Sie?"

Karog shook his head. "Nothing. Our patrol may have wounded a couple — but it was a brief contact. The jungle is a good friend of the hunted, Mr Cord." He sat back in his chair. "Now, to more direct business. First, the man who brought you here will be your guide tomorrow. He will meet you at nine a.m. outside your hotel. But the other point is less happy. Colonel Suramo asks that I tell you he has been in touch with Colonel Pappang, the commander of the Kuwa island garrison. Colonel Pappang is not inclined to give you permission to photograph the diamond pits — he will only do this if there is direct authorisation from Djakarta."

"That's awkward," Cord grimaced briefly. "Maybe if I talked to him . . . "

"I would not recommend it." Major Karog's manner hardened a little. "Pappang is not a man who changes his mind, nor is he so — so accommodating as Colonel Suramo. I must warn you, Mr Cord, that if you still attempt to go to Kuwa we cannot answer for your personal freedom."

"You mean Pappang might bounce me into a cell?"

"Until such time as he received instructions from Djakarta," nodded Karog sombrely.

"Well, you can't win all the time." Cord lifted the knife from the desk, slipped it into his pocket, then looked around the room. "I thought your office was out beside the colonel's."

"This is more convenient. The colonel has his duties and outlook, I have mine."

"And the radio masts?"

"One is ours, the other is the local public broadcasting station. It is — ah — useful having them under the same roof." He could imagine it was, especially in an area where more people could probably listen than read. But Karog's fingers had begun to fiddle impatiently with the papers in front of him. Cord got to his feet.

"Well, I know one man who'll be

135

happy to hear you've got some of the stuff back from Captain Muka's bunch," he declared brightly. "Does the *Tari*'s skipper know yet?"

Karog's face didn't change expression. "No, not yet, Mr Cord," he said cheerfully. "But it will be taken care of soon." He pressed a bell at the side of the desk, and the interview was over.

★ ★ ★

Peter Dimo was already back at the Harimau when Cord returned to the hotel. His thin, bespectacled face beamed when he answered Cord's knock on his room door.

"Hey, I thought you'd be in solitary by now!" He swept Cord with him into the room. "What happened?"

"I got this back." Cord showed him the knife, and told that part of the story. When he finished, Dimo raised an eyebrow.

"Well, Karog should be happy. But if Colonel Suramo knows about it he

136

said nothing — I spent most of the afternoon telling him what a fine big governor he was."

"Everything sorted out?" Cord crossed over to the window and looked out. Dimo's room, like his own, faced the front. A small squad of soldiers were marching past below . . . well, maybe marching wasn't the word. He grinned a little. The pace was closer to a lethargic slouch.

"More or less, I suppose." Dimo's voice held a guarded, vaguely puzzled note. "Copra cargoes can start moving next week. I thought he'd tussle over a couple of things I wanted, but they didn't seem to worry him."

"Been anywhere else?"

Dimo shook his head in a lazy negative and lowered himself on to the bed with a murmured satisfaction. "That was enough, the way I feel. What's the time?" Cord glanced at his watch and found the hands read later than he'd expected. "Close on six."

"Fine." Dimo stretched back. "Then

137

I'm going to catch up on some sleep. Eight o'clock for eating, okay?"

"Suits me." Cord left the young Malaysian and went into his own room. It looked the way he'd left it, at first glance. But when he checked the travel bag and camera equipment he wasn't disappointed. He'd had a visitor, someone who'd made a not particularly successful attempt to leave things as he'd found them. Two paces took him to the dressing table, then he gave a frosty grin of satisfaction. The Neuhausen and ammunition clips were still taped securely to their hiding place.

That mattered in more ways than one. The Neuhausen was as near to a good luck piece as Talos Cord possessed — Andrew Beck had made it a twenty-first birthday present, unorthodox but typical of the Field Reconnaissance chief's attitude to practicalities.

He sat on the bed, lit a cheroot and, once it was glowing, brought out the wallet he'd taken from Karog's sergeant in the alleyway. It was a cheap plastic job, with about two hundred rupiahs in notes in its main fold. He pushed the money in beside his own, laid the warrant card to one side, and checked the rest. It amounted to worthless, personal stuff. There was still the inner pocket. He slipped two fingers inside, felt a long strip of thick pasteboard, drew it out, and chewed gently on the cheroot, surprised.

How a sergeant of military police came to possess a membership card for the Tan Sallong Society was a question he'd have liked answered. The card was in green, with the crest of a crescent and three stars in one corner. He frowned over it for a moment, added it to the warrant card, and returned both to his inside pocket. Torn up small, the wallet and other papers were easy enough to dispose of in the washroom.

Cord flicked the ash from his cheroot, and lay back on the bed, hands behind his head. Maybe an infantry patrol had found that knife in a dead bandit's pack, maybe not. He watched the thick blue smoke curl towards the buckled plasterboard ceiling. Lies and evasions seemed well up the list in Barumma's stock-in-trade, but sooner or later the fact that the *Tari*'s captain was missing would have to become common knowledge. Then it would be interesting to see just how much was done about it.

A little before eight Cord rolled off the bed, splashed some tepid water on his face, knotted his tie, and went through to collect Dimo. They went down together, had a drink at the bar, and saw no trace of Karog's man. The bar was busier, the custom equally split between Europeans and Asiatics, most of the latter fat, smooth, expensively dressed individuals who were obviously no permanent part of Barumma society.

"Over there . . . " Dimo nudged him, his head indicating a table near the bar. Two of the outsiders were huddled close over a third man, thin and wizened, who was spilling tiny fragments of dull stone from a small leather pouch into his cupped hand.

"A little bit of warm-up trade for the big occasion?" Cord watched, seeing how the two potential buyers examined the uncut diamonds one by one, their faces devoid of expression. A few muttered words and only a few of the stones went back in the bag while some thick bundles of rupiah notes changed hands.

"One of the free-lance diggers from up-country," suggested Dimo. "They buy a licence and work some of the small deposits. There's no fortune waiting, but they make a living — though I wouldn't fancy working all day at the bottom of a ten foot hole in the mud, which is what most of them have to do." He stopped, looked past Cord, and sucked lightly on his teeth. "Now, here's something . . . "

Cord turned. A new party was entering the crowded room, with Doorn

Allat leading the way and, a surprise on its own, Kate Shellon and Sadiah close behind. Kate was still in the same green dress, a small jade pendant hanging from her neck on a delicate gold chain. Sadiah had changed into a self-coloured cream costume. A thin, raw-boned European in his early forties completed the group. Allat glanced around, saw Cord and Dimo, smiled, and guided the others towards them.

"*Selamat malam* . . . good evening, gentlemen," he said briskly. "A pleasure to see you again. Now, let me see — the ladies you know, of course. But this is a good friend of mine, Janos Manton. Janos manages the radio station here."

The rest of the introductions took a moment. Manton had fair, receding hair and a tired face, the eyes heavy and slightly watery. The dark blue bow tie at the neck of his crumpled white shirt had wilted to one side. When he spoke, his voice was slow and heavy.

"Finding your way around all right, Cord?"

"So far." Cord fought down an instinctive dislike of the man. "I was more or less next-door to your place this afternoon, having a talk with Major Karog." He glanced at the girls. "Seems an army patrol made contact with some of Captain Muka's gang."

Kate Shellon showed immediate interest. "Did they . . . "

"No. No sign of the old man they kidnapped." He gestured towards the bar. "Like to join us in a drink?"

Apologetically, Doorn Allat shook his head. "Would you forgive us? Janos is already late and we have still to eat. Perhaps we can take what you would call — ah — a raincheck?"

Cord nodded, and they moved on, disappearing through the door leading into the dining room. He heard Dimo sigh.

"What's wrong?"

"Every time I see that dark-haired little *gadis* she's in too big a hurry to stop," complained Dimo.

"They both get around," murmured

Cord. "What's Manton's background?"

"A refugee of some kind from somewhere in Europe." Dimo removed his spectacles, breathed on the lenses, and polished them for a moment on an edge of his handkerchief. "You'll find Mantons in plenty of places — started for Australia the hard way, island-hopping, and never got there." He replaced the spectacles and shrugged. "Well, they've got one good idea. I'm hungry."

They finished their drinks and went through. A waiter found them a small table near the back of the busy dining room, on the opposite side from where Allat had settled his party, and they ordered from the limited choice available. Service at their end of the room was slow. Halfway through what was supposed to be a medium-rare steak but tasted more like off-cut of old buffalo, Cord saw Allat's table being cleared and coffee served.

"Influence," grumbled Dimo. "When the diamond buyers come to town they act like they bought the place."

Cord grimaced, sawing again at the plate before him. "They can buy this part of it any time."

He gave up after another few mouthfuls. Across the room, Sadiah Beh leaned over, spoke briefly to Kate then got to her feet and, escorted by Manton, walked towards the door.

As they went out, Dimo swore under his breath. "Now what goes on?"

"Maybe she wants to record his voice for posterity." Cord grinned at the Malaysian's glare. "You said you wanted to catch up on your sleep — now's your chance for an early night."

"Huh." Dimo showed his disgust then sighed again. "Well, perhaps. Your luck seems better, anyway."

Cord followed his glance. Now Doorn Allat had risen from the table. He exchanged a last few words with Kate Shellon, bowed slightly, and then made towards the exit. The girl settled back, poured herself another cup of

145

coffee from the pot on the table, and seemed in no hurry to leave.

"I am the one who gets hit on the head by Muka's men. I am the one who decides on a girl who disappears every other moment," Dimo grumbled on to himself for a moment. "Well, what are you waiting for, an engraved invitation? Me, I'm giving up."

He pushed back his chair and left. Cord stayed where he was for a moment then got to his feet and crossed over to Kate Shellon's table.

"Looks like we've both been left on our own . . ." he began.

"Sit down," she invited, nodding towards one of the empty chairs. As he settled, she explained, "Sadiah's gone back with Manton to the radio station — she's interested in the technical facilities. In fact, even the things she can do with our recording gear keep amazing me."

"And Allat?" Cord put his question casually. "When'd you meet him?"

"At the radio station this afternoon

146

— Doctor Brink took us there to meet Manton."

"Well, the diamond trade is certainly here in strength," grinned Cord. "And as far as I can make out, there's enough bright stuff lying around Barumma to keep everybody happy."

"I know." She shook her head with something approaching disbelief. "It seems crazy, in a rundown place like this. But . . ." she laughed softly ". . . well, I wouldn't mind the odd sample, like a pair of diamond earrings."

Cord inspected the ears concerned with quizzical care. "Maybe someone will oblige. How's the ethnic research going?"

"Fine so far. The Dragon Dancers are what matter, of course, but there's a chance we'll get something else before then." She stubbed her cigarette and frowned earnestly. "Talos, ever heard of an old man called Pak Gadjal? He's a *guru* — a sort of mixture of prophet and teacher."

"Sounds like a top-line holy man," said Cord dryly. "You might have trouble there — some Muslim priests rate women as second class citizens, one stage below a good horse."

She shook her head. "No, he's not that kind — more a sort of local elder statesman. Doorn Allat says Gadjal keeps out of politics, but if he wanted he could shape things around here any way he chose. What matters to me is that he's a particular authority on local folk-stories . . ."

"When Borneo was young, the kind of thing you're after." Cord nodded. "Well, got it fixed to record him?"

"Let's say we've a good chance." She fingered the jade pendant at her neck. "Allat reckons he can arrange it. He knows the *guru* from some time back — in fact, he's gone to talk to him now, at some village a mile or two inland. I'd have gone too, but he said it was better if he tried alone."

"He's probably right." Cord took a

cheroot from his top pocket and rolled it experimentally between finger and thumb, appreciating the smooth, firm leaf. "What's your own programme?"

"Tonight?" She wrinkled her nose. "Nothing. Why?"

"The suggestions are limited," he admitted. "They come down to a choice between a few drinks at the bar or a walk along the harbour. I've no transport."

"And I've done enough walking for one day." Amusement in her eyes, she opened the handbag on her lap, reached in, then offered him a set of keys. "Doctor Brink loaned us a jeep. If you're interested, it's outside — I wouldn't mind a drive around."

"Bless the good doctor!" Cord grinned, took the keys, and saw her close the handbag. "When?"

"Now — once I get a coat, anyway." She rose to her feet. "You'll find the jeep across the street — it's painted black. I won't be long."

Cord escorted her through to the

149

hotel foyer, then, while she went up to her room, he lit the cheroot and went out into the street. The night had a faintly chill edge, but the sky above was a deep, dark blue, richly spangled with stars. A dog was yapping somewhere, and lights shone brightly near the harbour. But the rest of Barumma seemed to have pulled up the drawbridge for the night. He walked across to the jeep, climbed aboard, and slid in behind the steering wheel.

Mouth twisted a little, he hummed softly to himself. Temporarily, at least, Major Karog seemed to have called off the watchdogs, which could be because they'd something more important to do. But right now Cord felt more interested in why Allat should be so keen to help the girls. Rambling legends from a village *guru*, even one with a particular prestige, hardly fitted the context of the normal revolutionary pattern. Allat . . . somehow the diamond merchant should mean more than he did.

Light, quick footsteps came towards

150

him and he turned. Kate Shellon, in white military-style trenchcoat swinging loose from her shoulders, reached the jeep and swung herself smoothly into the passenger seat.

"Ready," she declared. "Which way are we heading?"

"Up towards the river." Cord leaned forward, started the engine, and fed it a fraction more throttle. "The road's reasonable — what I've seen of it, anyway."

They drove off through the quiet, darkened town, the night hiding its ugliness and gifting in place a dark, shadowed air of sleeping mystery. Here and there, the jeep's headlamps found the occasional handful of wandering citizens and once a two-man night patrol of military police stood frowning at a corner, watching them pass. Then they were on the outskirts, getting an occasional glimpse of the River Ular, its slow, oily water managing a dull sparkle in the moonlight.

"I was out here this afternoon," said

151

Cord, one hand on the wheel, the other resting lightly on the gear lever. "Thought I'd call in on Chou Sie's family, see if they needed any help." The house was a little way ahead and he gestured towards its pagoda roof. "That's the place."

"It looks nice." Kate Shellon sighed a little and burrowed slightly deeper into her coat. "How — I mean, what happened?"

"I saw his wife. She's just waiting and hoping." Cord increased the jeep's speed a little, and they swept past the house, round another bend. The road's surface was still reasonably good and the feel of the night air on his face was a pleasure on its own. "What happens to you once you're finished here? Back to Manilla?"

She nodded. "For a spell. After that, I don't know yet. I've some holiday time due. Maybe I'll take a trip to Europe or the States."

"More ethnic study?" he asked with a mock seriousness.

152

She chuckled. "That wasn't what I had in mind."

The last of the houses were behind them, the jeep's headlamps now lit a dark funnel of road through thickening foliage as they met the edge of the jungle, and a little way on ahead they came to a fork. The main highway swept inland, a lesser track bending right, closer to the river. He slowed, swung the wheel, and they took the right-hand way. It was bumpier, and a moment later a glimpse of yellow eyes was followed by a small, fast-moving shape darting across the track and disappearing into the bushes.

The river appeared again, close to the edge of the track. Suddenly, Cord frowned, knocked the little vehicle out of gear, and let it coast off the track, bumping to a standstill. He switched off the lights. Above the crackle of the cooling exhaust came the night sounds of land and water — a rhythm of singing crickets, occasional, unseen splashes, a steady chorus of croaking frogs, a night bird's screech.

"Well?" Kate Shellon turned a little towards him, a resigned, expectant note in her voice.

He leaned forward, arms across the steering wheel, and nodded up-river. "Look."

"Where?" Surprised, she frowned then saw for herself. There were lights on ahead, on their side of the river, lights which were moving and sometimes disappeared as if being shaded. "What about it?"

He shook his head for silence. What might have been a human voice sounded faintly against the background chorus and was answered by another. He wasn't sure if it was imagination, but he heard the quiet throb of a diesel engine somewhere among it all. At last, he turned to the redhead.

"One piece of advice I got was that this is a part of the world where you don't join a party without an invitation." He rubbed one hand along his chin. "Whoever they are, they're maybe quarter of a mile ahead. Mind if I take a look — alone?"

"And leave me here in the middle of this lot?" The prospect didn't appeal. "They're probably just a bunch of fishermen, minding their own business."

"Probably."

Something in his voice made her have second thoughts. "You mean you think . . ."

"I'm not thinking anything yet." He looked around. The jeep was sufficiently off the track to be hidden from most sides. "Come if you want."

"It's still none of our business but . . ." she shrugged and nodded.

They left the jeep and began walking along the edge of the track, towards the lights, the vegetation underfoot soft and spongy, small, invisible flying things brushing their faces. The girl swore softly as she half-tripped over a fallen branch, but he caught her arm and helped her on.

"Talos, I think this is a crazy idea," she protested, her voice a low hiss.

For answer, he held on to her arm and kept going forward. Then, at the next bend in the track, he stopped and his grip tightened.

"Now wha . . ." her voice died away as he pulled her back behind a tree.

On ahead, a hundred yards from where they stood, two men squatted beside the glow of a heavily shaded lantern. The light was poor, but enough to pick out the glinting rifle barrels across their knees. And behind the men, where the river bank widened into a small bay, the mystery of the lights was explained. The dark shapes of two large *kumpits* lay against the shore with a number of vehicles, two of them trucks, close beside them. Men were moving between the boats and the vehicles, working under the glow of other lanterns.

At last, he felt her nudge him. "What do we do now?" she asked quietly, her voice steady.

He shook his head, thinking. They were only a few miles out of Barumma and the men ahead could be anything from ordinary smugglers putting in a spot of overtime to a gang of coastal pirates newly returned from a raid. Only, the men working at the boats seemed to be loading them. . . . He turned, his lips close to her ear.

"I'll take a look."

Before Kate could answer, he was moving away, heading into the trees, circling the men on guard, moving at a crouch, cursing the hooked thorns which tugged at his clothing.

It took roughly three minutes to reach the place he wanted, on the very fringe of the jungle growth and less than twenty yards from the nearest truck. Cord inched forward on stomach and elbows until the tough river grass thinned then stopped, his mouth tightening.

Some of the men moving in the lantern light were in army uniform, others wore the dark green fatigue-type overalls he'd last seen when the *Tari* was boarded. Working in pairs,

157

they carried wooden boxes from the trucks to one of the *kumpits* while three men in civilian clothes stood beside a truck, watching. Two were immediately familiar, the man with the withered arm and his companion from the Tengah Import warehouse. The third figure was nothing more than a vague outline close under the shadow of the truck, probably around medium height.

A shout from one of the loading team signalled the last of the wooden boxes was going aboard. The trio by the truck stirred, and Cord tensed, hoping for a better view.

The whole picture froze as a single shot blasted out, followed seconds later by two more heavy reports in quick succession. He thought of Kate Shellon, felt suddenly sick in his stomach, then drew a deep breath as he realised the firing had come from the other end of the little bay. To his front, the reaction was immediate and without panic. A few, barked, staccato orders and a section of the army men had grabbed their weapons and were heading in the direction of the shots. The remainder spread out in a well-spaced defensive line while the *kumpit* crews swarmed aboard their vessels. Across the bay, sounding slightly further away, another shot cracked out, sharper, from a small calibre weapon, and was answered.

But the trio by the truck — Cord looked for them again and groaned his disgust. The truck was starting up. Still without lights, it began moving, swinging round on full lock, turning towards the road. He had a momentary glimpse of three figures in the cab, and then it was growling away, the Tengah Import sign on its side plain in the moonlight.

Shouts, and the noise of angry men beating their way through the bushes, made him realise a new danger. The other unknown watcher might try to double back and lead the pursuit straight towards him. Quickly, Cord wriggled back the way he'd come, got to his feet as soon as it was safe, and clipped a good thirty seconds off the return journey to where he'd left Kate.

Still hugging the shelter of the tree, the redhead jerked as if stung when he suddenly materialised beside her. Then she sighed with relief.

"I heard shots and — and then there was a truck . . . " she kept her voice low, and it trembled a little.

"They're after someone else," he said softly, edging forward to see along the track. The two guards were still there, on their feet now, rifles held at a nervous ready, liable to shoot at anything which moved. Gently, he inched back, touched her shoulder, and dumb-showed in the direction of the jeep. She needed no second telling.

When at last they reached it the little vehicle showed no sign of having had visitors. They climbed aboard and Cord slumped down, feeling the sweat beading his forehead. Upriver the last of the lights had vanished and there were no further shots.

"Now, if you don't mind me asking, what's going on back there?" Kate Shellon fumbled in her coat pocket, found her cigarettes, and placed one between her lips, fingers slightly unsteady. Cord found his lighter, snapped it to life, and shielded the flame closely between his hands while she bent forward.

"Trouble, the kind it is better to stay away from," he said grimly. "In a couple of minutes we take this jeep out of here and you forget the rest."

She drew hard on the cigarette, staring at him with eyes showing open amazement. "But — but we should tell Colonel Suramo, the military, somebody . . . "

"And you might be telling the wrong people for all we know." He put a harsh, deliberate emphasis behind the words. "Kate, I mean it. You came here to make some tapes at this Dragon Dance, festival — all right, make them. But then get out of this place, fast.

That's a friendly warning."

"I heard." Her hand cupped the cigarette's tiny glow and she looked away. "Talos, you — well, you're involved in what's going on?"

"On the fringe," he said shortly. "And you now know enough to land us both in a cell — if we got that far."

She took it calmly. "And you're no photographer. So Sadiah was right after all — and I told her she was being crazy when she wondered about you."

"Just keep on saying it, and make it convincing." Cord stopped and pointed silently out towards the river. Like two black ghosts, travelling under sail, not a light visible, the *kumpits* were moving down towards the sea. "Well, they've decided to leave."

"What about the men with the other trucks?"

He shook his head. "Probably heading inland — if they've given up looking for whoever they were after. I hope

162

he made it. We'll give them a little time."

Suddenly, he heard her giggle, a sound so strange that he wondered if it was a prelude to hysterics. But then he realised she was shaking with suppressed laughter.

"What's so funny?"

"Funny?" She stopped, shaking her head. "Nothing. But — but there's all this, and when you stopped the jeep I thought . . . "

Cord understood and grinned in turn. "I can guess."

She was watching him quizzically, saying nothing. He took the cigarette from her fingers and tossed it out of the jeep. Then he reached out, gripped her lightly by the shoulders, and brought her towards him. Kate's lips came up to meet his own. Mouth soft and willing, she made a gentle, sighing noise in her throat. The coat slipped from her shoulders, and her fingertips came up towards his cheek, stroking gently along the scar.

For a few seconds longer they stayed together then, slowly, she pulled away and brushed the hair back from her forehead. She smiled. "I'd still feel safer out of here."

He nodded, listened a moment, then started the jeep. The gear lever clicked smoothly into reverse and, keeping the engine note low, he backed the vehicle out of the bushes and on to the track.

Twenty minutes later, after an uneventful journey, they arrived back at the Harimau Hotel. A car was parked outside, and when they entered the building there was laughter coming from the bar.

Cord crossed over to the door, opened it a fraction, and looked in. Peter Dimo was there, sitting on a high stool, spectacles glinting, a broad grin on his boyish face while he launched out on yet another story. His audience was Sadiah Beh and the European from the radio station.

He closed the door gently, turned,

and went back to Kate. As they headed together towards the tiny elevator the Indian desk clerk watched them wearily for a moment then turned back to his book.

5

SOMEONE — either Colonel Suramo or Major Karog — had a warped sense of humour.

Promptly on nine a.m., while Talos Cord was finishing a lone, late breakfast of coffee and bread rolls in the dining room, a waiter came over and murmured he was wanted at the reception desk. Cord took another mouthful of coffee, gathered up the camera gear he'd left behind his chair, and went out. Karog's plain-clothes sergeant stood gloomily by the desk.

"*Salam, Tuan* Cord."

"Morning." Cord slung the camera strap over one shoulder. "Looking for me, Sergeant?"

"*Ja*." The man forced himself to look more friendly. "I have been assigned as your guide."

"Good!" Cord slapped him cheerfully

166

on the back. "Where do we start?"

"I have a car outside, and a list." His long face glumly resolved, the man led the way.

The car was an old, noisy Volkswagen with faded, torn upholstery and the sergeant handled it in a way that would have brought tears to the German builders. For the next three hours, while its interior grew more and more like an oven, his guide faithfully pencil-ticked in turn each stop on the typewritten list. Copra warehouses and timber yards, a medical centre built with American aid, a couple of schools — Cord winced at the fervour with which twelve-year-olds drilled with dummy rifles while his camera clicked on. Twice, between stops on the list, he had the sergeant halt the car. The first time, what looked like a crumbling old fortress turned out to be the local jail.

"*Tidak*." The man let him look, but shook his head determinedly at the suggestion of a photograph. "It is not approved."

The other halt met more enthusiasm once Cord said blandly that he wanted a close-up picture of his guide. The sergeant posed willingly, holding a fixed, gold-toothed smile. Cord made a pretence of deciding a camera angle. They were on a hill a short distance south of town, and the whole of Barumma, from harbour to riverside, was spread below like a relief map. But what held his attention lay further out, beyond the bulk of Kuwa island, close against the shore of its smaller neighbour, the Isle of Dragons. Sails lowered, two dark-hulled *kumpits* lay at anchor. A speck which might be a small boat was drawn up at the edge of the beach.

"*Tuan*?" The sergeant was anxiously civil.

"That's fine — just hold it like that." Cord raised his camera, clicked the shutter, and solemnly wound on the film to the next frame as they returned to the car.

Precisely at noon he was delivered

back to the Harimau. The sergeant switched off the car's engine, took out his list, and considered it earnestly. "*Sekarang* . . . now this afternoon it will be the turn of local industry . . . "

"Not for me," said Cord firmly. "I've had enough for one day."

The man looked anxious. "If there is something wrong . . ."

"Everything's fine. But no photographs this afternoon. I've got other plans. I'm going to enjoy myself. Know what I mean?"

Slowly, the sergeant's face thawed into a leer. "*Ja*. Perhaps there is a place I could suggest . . . "

"I've got something in mind." Cord got out then held the car door open for a moment. "One thing about tomorrow, though. I'd like to work in a little bit of local culture, present-day stuff. Know anything about this Tan Sallong Society?"

The leer vanished. The sergeant shook his head. "*Tuan*, I have heard of them. But they are men of learning,

169

and I am not. I cannot help."

"Don't worry about it." Cord closed the door and softly called the man a liar as the Volkswagen pulled away.

Inside the hotel, there was an unusual air of bustle around the reception area. Two army orderlies, complete with white shoulder lanyards and matching gloves, were waiting by the elevator. The Indian desk clerk had his jacket on and was hovering near while a cluster of guests had gathered in the background.

"The wanderer returns!" Peter Dimo's sardonic tenor made him turn. The young Malaysian lounged in an armchair a few feet away, a cigarette between his lips, a lazy grin on his face. "You're back in time to catch the last act."

"What goes on, Peter?" Cord dropped into the next chair. "Our young ladies. Or maybe I should say your one — I can't even get started with mine." Dimo's eyes twinkled knowingly through the spectacle lenses. "They've got the Old Man of the Woods up there, and he's getting the full V.I.P. welcome. First Major Karog turned up, scaring hell out of the staff, then the old boy arrives with Colonel Suramo and friend Allat, both treating him like visiting royalty."

"Pak Gadjal?" Cord blinked. "That's fast — Allat only went to see him last night."

"Did he?" Dimo shrugged, apparently disinterested. "Well, he must have been pretty persuasive. As far as I can make out they've been upstairs for a couple of hours now." He leaned back and blew a perfect smoke ring towards the ceiling. "What's your day been like?"

"The guided tour. Everything but the local sewage plant."

"They don't have one. Well, you missed another little item of news. Our captain of the *Tari* has disappeared. Gone, just like that." He snapped his fingers.

"What happened?"

"Nobody's sure. He just hasn't been seen since yesterday." Dimo stopped

171

and leaned forward a little. The elevator had come creaking down. One of the soldiers sprang forward, shouldering the desk clerk aside as the door rattled open. There were five people aboard, packed close together.

Colonel Suramo's bear-like shape was the first out. The district governor glanced at the nearest of his men, nodded, and the soldier hurried off towards the exit.

"Transport, at the double," murmured Dimo. "Well, there's the old Father Elephant himself — it you want the literal translation. Impressed?"

It was hardly the word. As Kate and Sadiah left the elevator they were followed by a bent, grey-bearded figure while Doorn Allat hovered in the background. Pak Gadjal might rank as the local father figure, but it was a long time since Cord had seen anyone with such an immediate magnetism — and so little to explain it. The old man was probably well in his eighties, wore native sandals with homespun pantaloons, a loose, long-sleeved white shirt and black waistcoat, and walked slowly with the aid of a neatly furled umbrella. The face was like wrinkled leather but under heavy white brows the eyes twinkled brightly as he talked to the girls.

Colonel Suramo saw them, nodded, left his charge, and came over.

"The arrangements are satisfactory, Mr Cord?"

"Everything fine," agreed Cord. "How'd the session go upstairs?"

"Excellent!" Suramo fingered the tips of his waxed moustache and beamed. "He is a wonderful old man, our Pak Gadjal. If any of us are like that at his age, we will have cause to be grateful." He took a step nearer. "I came to remind you about this evening's gathering. There will be a car sent to the hotel at eight — that will be suitable?"

"Couldn't be better," agreed Dimo from the background. "Having many people along, Colonel?"

"Various friends — you will meet them." The orderly had re-entered the hotel. Suramo saw him, nodded an abrupt farewell and hurried back to the elderly V.I.P.

Cord and Dimo stayed where they were, watching. Pak Gadjal had a last word with both girls then was carefully escorted out to the waiting car, Suramo and Doorn Allat one on either side. The rest of the spectators began to disperse. Cord got to his feet, and went over.

"Hello, Kate."

"Talos!" For the first time he noticed how her eyes crinkled when she smiled. "I didn't see you."

"We were well out on the fringe," he said dryly. "How'd it go with him?"

"He's fantastic," she declared enthusiastically. "I feel like we've found a walking encyclopaedia on local folklore — stories, legends, ballads, the lot. And we only started to scratch the surface. I need time with him, a lot of time."

"Time's always precious," he agreed neutrally.

Kate's expression changed a fraction at the underlying warning then, quickly, she turned to her companion. "Sadiah, how about recording quality?"

"Should be good. For an old man he's got a strong voice, strong and clear." Though she spoke to Kate, the girl's eyes were on Cord, her attitude strangely speculative. It left him wondering how much she guessed, how much she knew about the previous night.

"You think it's good?" queried Dimo, arriving at her side. "Then how about letting us hear a sample?"

"*Entah* . . . I don't know." Sadiah's snub nose wrinkled and she frowned uncertainly. "It's really up to Kate, and the tapes aren't sorted out in any way . . . "

"Just as a favour?" Dimo gave the redhead an appealing, lop-sided grin. "Then afterwards we can get Talos to buy us all lunch, eh?"

175

"Well . . . " Kate shrugged good-naturedly " . . . all right. I'd like to hear a little of it myself, just to make sure. Let's go up. Colonel Suramo fixed things with the management, and we had an extra room to ourselves as a studio for this morning."

They didn't bother with the elevator and walked the one floor up. The temporary 'studio' looked like part of the manager's private apartment, furnished as a lounge, the recorder and microphone still lying on a small table, reels of tape, spare dry batteries and other equipment scattered around.

"I'll need a minute or so," warned Sadiah. "The reels are still all tail-out — I'll need to run one back." With quick, expert fingers she fed one of the reels into the machine, flicked switches, and the golden-brown recording tape began whirling.

"How many reels did you use?" queried Cord.

"Four — high speed, high quality," replied Sadiah absently, watching the

176

speeding spindles. "This is the last of them."

"You're sure it was just four? — I thought . . . " Kate Shellon stopped and shook her head. "I suppose I lost count. My job was to keep him talking." She glanced at Cord and confessed. "It was a problem on its own. Most of the time I had to fall back on Colonel Suramo as interpreter."

Dimo murmured sympathetically. "No one would call Indonesian an easy language, least of all the Indonesians. Often enough they can't understand each other — there are over two hundred dialects."

The tape was ready. Sadiah pressed the play-back button and immediately a rich, calm voice came from the recorder, filling the room. She adjusted the volume a little and stood back.

Cord listened, concentrating hard, catching the main thread but finding it hard to translate much of what the old man was saying. The story was one almost as old as time — of a child stolen from its mother by earth spirits, then returning years later to the tribe with strange, magical powers. The voice chuckled occasionally, then changed mood to match the telling, words flowing without hesitation. Once or twice, when Pak Gadjal did stop, he heard Kate and Suramo in the background, a question asked, and then the story threads continued.

"That'll do for now." Kate stepped forward and switched off the recorder. "Talos, suppose you go down while Sadiah and I tidy this lot away. Have a drink or something. We won't be long."

★ ★ ★

The meal passed quickly, its main feature Peter Dimo's persistent, bantering, but not particularly successful verbal assault on Sadiah's defences. The plump Indonesian girl showed she had a tongue which could at least match his own, leaving Kate and Cord reduced to mere spectators.

At last, Kate sighed a little and looked at her watch. "We'll have to go. Doctor Brink is expecting us. It's a final talk about the Dragon Dance arrangements."

"How long now?" queried Dimo.

"Tomorrow night," said Cord then added casually, "looks like they're getting organised already. I saw a couple of boats lying off the island this morning, unloading."

"That's right," agreed Sadiah, apparently eager to switch to a topic other than herself. "Kate saw them too. The colonel told us they were landing provisions and other stuff — even dancers have to eat."

"And even I have to earn a living," grinned Dimo, pushing back his chair. "I've people to see, things to do. What about you, Talos?"

"The same." Cord signalled the waiter, signed for the bill, and they broke up.

He left the Harimau about half an

hour later and headed for the harbour by a roundabout way which gave him ample time to make sure he wasn't being followed. Once there it didn't take long to find what he wanted, a medium-sized fishing canoe moored beside the pier with a handy outboard motor at her stern and the owner aboard, mending a net. It needed a surprisingly few rupiah notes to strike a bargain, then he was aboard, sitting beneath a small hooped shelter of matting, and the canoe was throbbing its way out to sea.

The fisherman, young, his jaws moving rhythmically as he chewed on a wad of betel nut, followed his instructions to the letter. The canoe held a steady course well clear of the shore of Kuwa Island until the narrow gap between Kuwa and the Isle of Dragons became visible, showing the narrow causeway linking the two blobs of land.

"*Tuan*?" The fisherman raised a questioning eyebrow.

Cord nodded, the outboard's tiller swung, and they gradually closed in until they were plugging along in a gentle, rolling swell less than a hundred yards off the sandy edge of the Isle of Dragons.

The *kumpits* had gone, which didn't surprise him. At one point on the beach he saw marks which might have been where a heavily laden boat was dragged up above high-water mark. He made a mental note of the spot and kept watching. But the rest was empty beach, drab scrub and a few handfuls of unhappy looking palm trees.

The swell increased a little as they turned the final point of the island. The canoe began bobbing, taking an occasional drenching of fine spray, and once again the story was the same — empty beach, no sign of life. As they neared Kuwa once more, the fisherman began to ease his little craft further out.

Cord sat silent, lips pursed, seeing the small landing stage which jutted out from the diamond island about a quarter mile further on. He'd come this far . . .

"*Disitu* . . . " He met the boatman's puzzled gaze and pointed again. "*Disitu* . . . over there."

The man frowned unhappily. Carefully, watching him, Cord counted out another little pile of rupiah notes, stopped, and waited. The man muttered something to himself, gave a resigned shrug, and took the money.

Five minutes later, they bumped alongside the landing stage and Cord stepped ashore under the stony-faced gaze of two carbine-armed soldiers.

"*Salam* . . . it is important I talk to Colonel Pappang."

Neither face moved a muscle. One carbine stayed centred on Cord's middle, the other was trained on the canoe.

At last, a new figure hurried on to the landing stage. The lieutenant was plump, flustered, and still fastening the buttons of his tunic. Cord repeated his request.

"*Boleh djadi* . . . perhaps, but it is not so simple." The lieutenant scowled, tugged pensively at his lower lip, then marched towards a small hut at the shore end of the landing stage. A telephone wire ran from its roof. He went inside, was gone for a couple of minutes, and when he returned his manner was a fraction friendlier.

"Colonel Pappang will see you." He waved the carbines aside and allowed himself a grin. "We have heard of you, Mr Cord — you will notice we even know your name, though you have no camera. On Kuwa, we know most things that happen over in Barumma."

Cord allowed himself to be shepherded away from the guards and his fisherman to where a small pick-up truck was parked. The lieutenant waved Cord aboard then climbed into the driving seat. The engine fired, and they started off along the narrow track.

Almost as soon as they were out of sight of the sea the landscape altered in fantastic fashion. Cord stared at the scene, fascinated. All around, like some rust-brown Lunar nightmare, the earth was studded with small, man-made craters, each surrounded by its spoil of sandy soil and rocks. Teams of ragged, mud-smeared men and women worked around them, some shifting more spoil as they deepened their particular hole, others working with planks, buttressing the soft earth sides.

Here and there, other equally mud-smeared figures were trudging with gravel-filled buckets on shoulder yokes, heading towards the only semi-mechanised units in the whole primitive complex — a few galvanised water tanks fed by small pump engines. Around the tanks, earlier arrivals were panning their gravel in gold-mining style.

"*Ja*, it surprises most people, Mr Cord." The soldier read his expression and chuckled. "There are machines we could use, but we prefer not — and the returns are just as good. You would like to see a pit close-up?"

Cord nodded. The pick-up halted at the next of the craters lying near the track.

They got out and walked over. The hole was about twelve feet wide and apparently deserted. But, as they neared it, Cord heard a rhythmic scraping sound coming from its depths. He stood on the lip and looked down. A rough bamboo ladder was propped against one side of the hole and at the bottom, perhaps fifteen feet below ground, a muddy figure squatted on a thin layer of fine gravel, patiently scooping it into a collection of buckets at his side. The man was naked except for a pair of ragged shorts, and the bottom of the pit, obviously close on sea level, was damp and wet.

"*Hai*! You have a visitor," announced the lieutenant.

"Ah!" The miner sat back on his heels, grinning up at them, and answered in a dialect which was strange to Cord. The lieutenant laughed, shook his head, then gestured Cord back towards the pick-up.

He chuckled again as he started the vehicle. "He wanted to know if you'd come to finish the rest of his shift."

"Down there?" Cord grimaced at the thought. "No thanks."

"They are paid well by their standards," protested the soldier. "That man, for instance, may find five diamonds today or may find none — but either way he draws the same wage. Is that not what your Western experts would call social justice?"

It seemed best not to follow that one. Cord let him concentrate on driving, and they passed still more of the craters until they bucked over a small rise in the ground and came down towards a cluster of barrack-like single-storey huts. The few figures in sight were in uniform, and the pick-up stopped outside a brick-built block which had all the appearance of a miniature fortress.

Once again, his escort led the way, past an armed sentry, down a short corridor, and into Colonel Pappang's outer office. A clerk with a holstered sidearm sprang to his feet, rapped on a glass door, then waved them through.

Inside, Cord stopped short. The diamond isle's commandant was standing beside a narrow window-slit, a small, thin man with broad cheekbones and slightly protruding front teeth. Narrow-shouldered, young, it seemed wrong he should be in any kind of uniform. But Pappang's eyes and aloof bearing made it clear a hasty judgment could be wrong.

"Mr Cord?" The voice was cool and slightly irate. "Lieutenant Maung tells me you landed without permission. Why?"

Cord shrugged. "It seemed as good a way as any to see you."

The tight lips parted in a suspicion of amusement. "*Astaga* . . . there are more usual ways."

"And I tried them. Colonel Suramo passed the message that you didn't want me. I decided to find out why."

"I see." It came as a soft hiss.

Pappang glanced at his subordinate and jerked his head towards the door. As the man went out, Pappang leaned back against the window-slit. "Would it surprise you if I said there was no such message, Mr Cord?" He chewed thoughtfully, almost distastefully, at the nail of one thumb. "I was advised you were in Barumma — to that extent, at least, Suramo and I were in contact. But no request was made on your behalf."

"Then I'll be polite and call it a misunderstanding by someone." Cord glanced around. The Commandant's office was very much a workroom, sparsely furnished, its major item a bulky metal safe with a heavy, triple-locked door. "Suppose I make the request now?"

"It will still be turned down. To that extent, at least, Colonel Suramo was correct." The small, thin soldier glared challengingly at him. "Mr Cord, I understand that even your presence in Barumma is questionable, due in part to outside influence. But Kuwa is not in the sphere of influence of the Rajah-Laut Agencies — or that of any other commercial concern. It is a security restricted area under my separate command." The teeth clicked their distaste. "The fisherman who brought you was paid well?"

"I thought so," agreed Cord calmly. "Colonel, all I want to do is take some pictures when the diamond auction is in progress . . ."

"Impossible." Pappang crossed to his desk, sat down, and hunched forward, his manner grim. "Mr Cord, I will give you the benefit of not appreciating what you have done by landing here. But let me explain that on Kuwa we discourage contact with the outside world. The reason is obvious, the risk of diamond smuggling. Our workers, like my men, are from outside this area — deliberately. The workers serve their contract without leaving the island, my men do likewise, and our supplies coming in over the causeway or by sea are all the contacts we desire."

"You make it sound like a branch of the county jail," mused Cord. "Nobody complains?"

"A few, with reasons of their own. Two of them were shot a few months ago, smuggling out a parcel of stones." Pappang gave a sigh. "And, of course, they complain in Barumma — they always complain in Barumma."

"I know the Dragon Dancers are fairly peeved," nodded Cord. "They say you're making things difficult."

"Perhaps." Pappang looked away from him. "I am in charge of a ridiculous little island which is mostly mud-holes. And Indonesia has thousands of other islands, all trying to become a single nation." Suddenly, he swung round and pointed to the safe. "The idiocies of our politicians at Djakarta don't concern me, Mr Cord. Inside that safe is what I have to guard — the harvest from our mud-holes. *Masja Allah*, it is a good harvest too. In rupiahs . . . no, let us be more realistic, and talk in dollars. There are diamonds in there worth perhaps twenty million dollars, give or take the odd million. I will have a more exact idea after tomorrow night when the diamond merchants have had their preview."

"Well, I wouldn't haggle over the odd million," murmured Cord. "I know someone who'd be happy enough to get just two stones from that lot. But . . . you're having your preview on the same night as the Dragon Dances?"

"Not from choice. My date was fixed first, the other depends on such things as phases of the moon and auspicious signs." Pappang's disgust was clear.

"But I still can't take pictures?"

"No." It was flat and final. "Mr Cord, I take it Colonel Suramo is unaware of this visit?"

Cord nodded. "I thought it was better that way."

"And I think it should stay so, for reasons of my own." Pappang glanced again at the safe and his lips pursed briefly. "You may be interested in our security system. Among other things, this room is guarded night and day. The sentries have orders to shoot on sight if any — ah — unauthorised visitor is found near it."

"I'll remember," promised Cord wryly.

"Good. You will be returned to your boat. I regret we will not meet again." Pappang pressed the buzzer on his desk.

★ ★ ★

One considerably shaken fisherman steered the canoe back alongside Barumma's pier an hour later, accepted some further rupiahs to help soothe his nerves, and promptly settled back to repairing his nets with a new, thankful enthusiasm.

Cord walked thoughtfully through the dusty, sun-baked streets, heading for the Harimau. He'd gained a new respect for the flat monotony of Kuwa island — and had an equal respect for its thin, earnest commander. Pappang had all the hallmarks of an honest, go by the book soldier, which was probably why he'd been chosen for the job.

Kuwa mattered, in a way which threw an entirely new significance on any upsurge of revolt in this part of Borneo. It might also place a diamond buyer like Doorn Allat in a new importance — and perhaps even make sense of why another diamond merchant had had to be kidnapped. And, on a minor key, why had Suramo been so anxious to keep him from going to visit the opposition colonel?

Still mulling it over, he pushed his way through the hotel's swing doors and crossed the foyer. Then he stopped, vaguely conscious that the desk clerk was trying to attract his attention.

"Mr Cord — it is for you," repeated the Indian patiently, waving a small envelope. "A *tilgram*. It arrived about an hour ago."

Cord took the envelope, thanked him, and collected a bottle of beer from the bar before he went up to his room. Then, the door closed, the beer uncapped, he took a long, thankful swallow of the tepid liquid and opened the cable. Wryly, he reminded himself that a copy was probably on Suramo's desk — if in fact the original hadn't gone there first. But either way was safe enough. Field Reconnaissance avoided code most of the time, preferred to send plain language messages which allowed their men to read between the lines, even though it sometimes meant involved intellectual exercise.

This one read innocently enough, a minor rocket from employer to employee.

LATEST PIC-BATCH RECEIVED. SHORT ON IMPACT PERSONALITY COVERAGE. MISSING FROM BROADER FIELD. SUGGEST FILL GAP BY SERIES YOUR PRESENT LOCATION.

It was signed by a non-existent picture editor. But the Singapore agent who'd drafted it couldn't have been more explicit. A number of key trouble-makers scattered over different locations in South East Asia were suddenly dropping out of sight, a sure sign crisis temperature was rising. And the reasons were liable to be found in Barumma.

Sheer habit made him tear up the cable and dispose of it via the washroom. He drank more of the beer, noticed a couple of large black flies buzzing near the window, and patiently stalked each in turn with the heel of one shoe. His shirt had long since stuck to his back with perspiration and his head was like tight-packed cottonwool. Wearily, he dropped on to the bed, tried to think for a spell, and finally gave up.

When he wakened, it was coming on for dusk. Cord yawned, rolled off the bed, and headed for the shower. He came out still wet, let his body dry itself, chose the last of his clean shirts and found his only tie. Somehow, he had the feeling Suramo's party might require a little extra attention. Frowning, he crossed to the dressing table, retrieved the Neuhausen and its clips, and stowed the gun in an inside pocket of his jerkin. Using the little Swedish knife, he cut some fresh lengths of camera tape and taped the spare clips to the inside of his left leg, just below the knee. Grinning at his reflection in the fly-blown mirror, he finished dressing, picked up the twin-reflex camera, and headed down towards the bar.

Peter Dimo was already there, entrenched behind a tall glass of whisky and water. He greeted Cord cheerfully, ordered him the same, and settled back.

"Any sign of the girls?" Cord glanced at his watch. It was close on eight and Suramo's car would be arriving soon.

"Despite signs to the contrary, you know little about women when you ask that kind of question," said Dimo solemnly. He sipped his drink. "It is part of Allah's plan that all women should be unpunctual — or, if you want it in plain language, only fifteen minutes ago I saw Sadiah come hammering in from the street like she was being chased. So, as is also part of Allah's plan, we sit and are patient."

The promised car, with an n.c.o. driver, arrived outside the hotel exactly on eight. After another ten minutes, Cord and Dimo moved out into the main foyer — and at last the elevator squeaked down. Dimo whistled a soft appreciation as the girls stepped out. Sadiah Beh wore a plain, square-necked dress of pure white without sleeves, gathered at the waist by a softly tanned leather belt. Her raven hair was piled high on her head, and jewellery was restricted to a pair of heavy, swinging silver ear-rings. Beside her, a study in contrast, her red hair brushed back and gleaming in the overhead light,

Kate Shellon's dress was a straight cut linen shift, a sheath of pastel green, the jade pendant lying in the hollow of its scooped neckline.

"We're late," said Kate apologetically.

"I was, anyway," qualified Sadiah. "The car . . ."

"Is outside." Dimo was suddenly in no hurry. "You move fast, little one — I saw when you got back."

"I was working," said the girl, slightly on the defensive. "I lost track of time."

"Which is Sadiah's weakness," agreed Kate, smiling at Cord. "Next time she goes near that radio station I'll tie an alarm clock round her neck."

"Back there again?" Cord raised an eyebrow. "What's the attraction?"

"I was listening to some tapes from Janos Manton's library . . . " began Sadiah.

"They've quite a collection of native music," nodded Kate, helping her out. "Manton says we can copy a few, and Sadiah's doing the selecting."

198

"With Manton?" Dimo shook his head. "Then she has my sympathy."

"Why?" demanded Sadiah, surprised.

He grinned. "Well, for a start, you could have been with me instead. But not listening to tapes!" He took her arm, and started for the door.

In the car, on the way to Suramo's country-house head-quarters, Dimo clowned happily in the back seat with a girl on either side of him. His stories kept coming like water from a tap and up front, listening, Cord saw their driver frown uncertainly at the gurgling laughter. The last and longest, involving a missionary and a tiger that stopped to say grace, finished as the car swept in through the guarded gate in the fence and slowed to stop outside the long, rambling house's lighted doorway, where the inevitable sentry was posted.

As they got out, Major Karog appeared beside the sentry and greeted them with a determinedly cheerful smile on his broad, high-cheeked face.

"*Selamat datang* . . . welcome, ladies!" He glanced at Cord and Dimo with slightly less enthusiasm. "I see you have a camera, Mr Cord . . . "

"I can leave it." Cord hefted the twin reflex by its strap. "It's just in case the colonel's in a mood for having a picture taken."

"Perhaps." Karog swept one arm in an invitation. "Now, if we are ready . . . "

They followed him into the house then along a different corridor from the one Cord had travelled on his previous visit. Suddenly, they found themselves in a broad, richly carpeted room, softly lit from a central glass chandelier, the air already blue with tobacco smoke, about a score of people standing around. All were talking, most had filled glasses in their hand.

"Ah!" Colonel Suramo, resplendent in a tightly buttoned dress tunic, a rash of medals on one breast, emerged from one little cluster and came towards them. "So now we are complete, eh,

Karog? No need to send out that patrol you were threatening."

They murmured apologies, but one massive paw dismissed the idea. "Miss Shellon, I am particularly pleased you and your friend could come. There are several people here who wish to meet you. Now . . . " he glanced at Karog. "Major, while I conduct Miss Shellon and Miss Beh round the other guests, you can take care of Cord and Dimo. Understood?"

Karog gave a reluctant nod. "Colonel, Mr Cord has brought a camera . . . "

"I hardly thought it was a bomb," grunted Suramo. "Well, Mr Cord, what do you wish to see through your lenses this time?"

"You, when you've a moment," said Cord placidly.

"Hmm." The district governor showed no dislike of the idea. "Later, perhaps. I have my guests now, a small item of business afterwards — but I will let you know." He turned to the girls. "Now, to start, if like most of your sex you are interested in diamonds we have some experts here . . . "

Shepherded by Karog, Cord and Peter Dimo found themselves going off on an opposite course. A few of the hands they shook belonged to familiar faces like Doctor Brink and the pale, insipid Manton from the radio station. Two Dutch plantation managers, a cluster of up-country landowners with wives in long silk skirts and wide-sleeved, elaborately embroidered blouses, and a series of soft-voiced, bright-eyed diamond buyers made up the rest. Karog finished, snapped his fingers at a waiter, rammed a glass of pink, sherbet-flavoured soda water at each of them and quickly excused himself.

Dimo sipped and grimaced. "Official reception stuff. I might have known."

"Maybe it's good for the liver," said Cord absently. He glimpsed Kate's red hair over on the other side of the room, heard Suramo's voice booming from the same direction, but one person was surprisingly absent. He'd figured Doorn Allat as an automatic choice for the colonel's guest list, but so far there was no sign of the burly, smooth-spoken diamond buyer.

Dimo had struck up conversation with one of the plantation men. Quietly, carrying his glass like a membership badge, Cord eased over towards a nearby trio of diamond traders. They broke off their own discussion and greeted him with polite, cautious smiles, an intruder but no rival in their dealings.

"You're one short, aren't you?" he asked conversationally, then blinked apologetically. "Sorry, that's probably the awkward thing to say. I didn't mean the fellow who was grabbed from the *Tari*. I was thinking of Doorn Allat. Where is he? Out on Kuwa on his own, stealing a march?"

The nearest of the three, light-skinned and butter-fat, laughed briefly and without humour. "Of that there is no fear, Mr Cord. Colonel Pappang allows no one a sight of the stones until the official preview. Though . . . " he glanced significantly at his companions " . . . people have tried."

"Allat will be along soon," volunteered one of the others. "He was detained on some personal matter."

"Good — I wondered." Cord propped himself against the back of an over-stuffed couch. Like most semi-official gatherings, though there were plenty of chairs around few were in use. "He's from Sumatra, I know. Big firm?"

The gold teeth flashed momentarily at such innocence. "Let us say one in good standing, Mr Cord. In the *berlian* trade most firms are small, often one-man operations. It is trading results which matter."

Cord nodded casually. "You make it sound like a club. How long has Allat been a member?"

The third man, hitherto silent, shrugged a little. "His agency is old-established, of course. But he is fairly new. I think — yes, it is about two years since he took over the business from a European, and longer since anyone from Sumatra last came to the Barumma auction."

"So it's his first time here." Cord sipped the glass. "Nobody's met him before?" He stayed quiet as, in turn, the three men looked at one another and shook their heads. Then he shook his head admiringly and grinned at them. "Well, good luck at the auction."

He moved on, past the up-country landlords and their twittering, heavily-perfumed wives, gradually working his way towards Kate Shellon.

"Well now, Mr Cord . . ." a hand fell on his arm, and Doctor Brink's bright blue eyes twinkled at the sight of the drink in his hand " . . . enjoying yourself?"

"This?" Cord spoke with some feeling. "I've tasted more potent stuff in your country, doctor. Good lemon gin, then a chilled beer to wash down one of those Haringsla salads."

"Ah." The sun-dried face twitched

a little. "I have not forgotten — but there are some compensations out here, especially the next morning."

"True enough." Cord chuckled in turn. "How's everything out at the Isle of Dragons? All set for the big day?"

"There is little that can be done in advance, but what is possible is ready." The old Dutchman nodded happily. "The first of the people should begin arriving here in the morning. You will be with us in the evening? Colonel Sumaro has indicated he is hopeful . . ."

"He hasn't spoken to me yet, but I'd like it." A little to their left, Kate had joined Sadiah and both girls were talking to the pale-faced Janos Manton. Cord excused himself, left the doctor, and went over.

"Who's looking after the shop tonight, Manton?" he asked cheerfully.

"I have a competent staff, Mr Cord." The station manager regarded him coldly. "Routine programme work doesn't require my supervision."

"Any chance of seeing over your place sometime?" Cord winked at Sadiah. "From what I hear, you've quite a collection of tapes stored away. And I'd like to hear this ballad of Tan Sallong that seems to be top of the local pop parade."

"The ballad is hard to avoid. Every request programme carries it. The visit . . . " Manton shrugged. "In a few days perhaps. I will arrange something." Deliberately he turned away. "Sadiah, there is one point I would like to discuss with you . . . "

Left suddenly alone with Kate Shellon, Cord shrugged ruefully. "Well, what made me so popular?"

"I suppose he's got problems." She bit lightly on her lip, took a half-step closer, and dropped her voice to little more than a murmur. "Talos, did you know that Captain Chealu has disappeared? I've just heard."

Watching the others around, his face not changing expression, he nodded and told her softly, "It's permanent. I found him."

"Then . . . " she stopped and drew a breath. "But why? What's it all about?"

Cord shook his head. "Kate, I'm still trying to find out. But if the lid pops off things, you keep clear. Understand?" Suddenly, he raised his voice again as a uniformed figure bored towards them. "Anyway, I'm getting some good pictures. And — hello, Major Karog!" He greeted the soldier with masterly surprise. "Nice party — looking for someone?"

"Both of you," said Karog, his voice surprisingly civil. "Mr Cord, the colonel has some business to attend to at the moment. But he suggests that in half an hour he will be at your camera's disposal. Now, if I could have a moment with Miss Shellon to find out about her next recordings?"

"Help yourself. I'll circulate a little." Cheerfully, he turned away.

The talk was loud as ever, the

coloured soda water in plentiful supply. But Suramo's bulky figure wasn't the only one suddenly missing. Cord checked again, collided with one of the up-country wives, apologised, then laid his glass on a table, cursing his own blind stupidity. Manton had vanished, and so had Peter Dimo.

Add Doorn Allat's non-arrival and something was happening, happening now. Gently, unobtrusively, Cord worked his way to the door and slipped out into the empty corridor.

Colonel Suramo had 'a little business' to attend to — Cord guessed it might be his business too.

6

THE office area of the vast, rambling district headquarters was quiet, empty, and almost devoid of lights. Moving silently, keeping to the darker shadows, Talos Cord worked his way in the general direction of Colonel Suramo's room. Every sense he possessed was on the alert — just one mistake would be enough, and he'd few illusions about the consequences.

The next corridor looked familiar and a faint glow came from beyond a turning at the far end. He approached the glow with care, edged the last inches pressed against the wall, and took a quick glance round. Less than ten feet away a small electric bulb burned above Suramo's office door. Underneath it, an unlit cigarette dangling from his lips, his good hand significantly deep in his jacket pocket, the man with the withered arm leaned casually against the doorframe.

Gently, Cord tip-toed back. His shoulder brushed against a door and he stopped, trying to work out the geography involved. If he was right — he tried the door's handle and it turned easily, the hinges opening with the softest of squeaks. Inside, he closed the door again and, as his eyes became adjusted to the deeper gloom, saw he was in what looked like an orderly's cubicle. A thin crack of light ran across the floor a few feet ahead, light which came from under another door, a door which could only lead into Suramo's room.

Moving gingerly, aware of a vague murmur of sound coming from the other side of that door, he started towards it — then froze, heart thumping, right hand reaching instinctively towards the Neuhausen, as the camera slung over his shoulder slammed against the edge of a small desk. The twin reflex's leather carrying case absorbed most of the blow, but the sound still seemed horrifyingly loud.

For more than a minute he stayed rigid. But the murmuring voice didn't stop, the absolute quiet within the little cubby-hole was broken only by his breathing. Slowly, he brought his left hand back, gripped the camera, and held it firm. Then, with a sigh of relief, he took another step forward and was at the door. Like the rest of the building, it was old and solid — which offered its own possibility. Running his fingers down the edge, he found the round shape of a keyhole cover, twisted it open, and crouched down to peer through.

The view was narrow and restricted, yet enough. There were five men in the room, two of them strangers, small, wiry Asiatics in ill-fitting civilian suits. The others were Suramo, with his tunic unfastened, Doorn Allat, who had a cigar clamped in his mouth, and Manton. They were grouped around a table, and it was from the table that the voice was coming, where a tape machine was working. That rich, deep tone . . . suddenly, he placed it. Pak Gadjal! But the quiet words were no longer those of a revered *guru* from some village sanctuary recalling ancient legend. This was a man declaring sad anger, demanding support . . .

Doorn Allat bent forward, switched off the machine, laid down the cigar, then smiled at the others. When he spoke, his voice was so low that Cord had to concentrate every fibre to hear and understand.

"You and the girl have done a good job, Manton. This part is ready." He glanced at the others. "And at the island?"

"*Tamat* . . . it is finished," contributed one of the strangers, grinning. "The dragons will roar."

"And loudly," growled Colonel Suramo, scratching at his throat. "Loudly enough to be heard where it matters."

"Good." Allat clapped his hands

together in a gesture of satisfaction. "My own arrangements are made for exactly five minutes later."

A little less concentration on that awkward, ridiculous keyhole and Cord might have heard the soft whisper of the door behind him, perhaps even the rustle of clothing. But he hadn't. Instead, there was the click of a switch, the orderly's cubbyhole was suddenly bathed in light and, simultaneously, more telling than any words, a hoarse, baiting, laugh.

Very deliberately, he let his hands spread out from his side, rose slowly from his crouched position, and looked round. The broad, coarse face in the doorway sneered derisively while the man trained a heavy Mauser pistol unwaveringly at Cord's middle. Given any kind of an invitation, this was an animal which would kill and gain pleasure from the act.

"*Hai* . . . a visitor!" The withered arm jerked abruptly. "Go through then, foolish one."

Sighing, Cord obeyed. He'd come up against a professional. The thump of the camera case had been enough, but this man had known to wait before he acted.

The sight of the door swinging open brought every head in the room snapping round. As Cord walked in, his captor close behind, fear flickered on Janos Manton's face. But the others . . . Cord looked, and read only tense, questioning anger.

Inevitably, it was Allat who recovered first. "You, Mr Cord — this is a surprise!" The bland voice steadied and hardened. "Where did you find him, Palu?"

The muzzle of the Mauser jammed into Cord's back, pushing him further forward. "At a keyhole, Captain. I thought you would want him first . . ."

Allat nodded, and pursed his lips. "Well, Mr Cord, what brought you here, peeping through this keyhole?"

"The colonel wanted pictures, and I just came looking." Cord tried to grin convincingly and tapped the camera. "Then — well, I just became curious."

He didn't expect to be believed. But, for the moment, something else mattered. The man behind him had called Allat 'captain'. He tried to imagine the immaculately dressed diamond buyer in a set of loose, dark green overalls, to substitute the cool, bland features for a shapeless veil of gauze. So many little things about Allat's appearance and build, even the way he walked, had nagged at his memory, and now he realised why. He'd found the ghost-like Captain Muka. Only it didn't look as though the fact was going to be of much use.

"You became curious, Mr Cord." Wordlessly, Allat nodded to one of the strangers. The man padded forward, searched Cord's pockets, found the Neuhausen, and brought it back to Allat. Allat handed it in turn to Colonel Suramo, who swore heavily and tossed it on the table.

"Few people bring a gun to a social

gathering," mused Allat. "Perhaps you have an explanation there too?"

"Not without notice." Ignoring the gun behind him, Cord strolled nearer the table but far enough away from the Neuhausen to be sure his motive wasn't mistaken. "Looks like I broke up a private meeting."

"*Setan* . . . how much of this do we listen to?" For Suramo, it was too much already. He took two lumbering steps forward, his arm swung, and Cord winced at the heavy, backhand blow which took him across the mouth. The district governor turned to Allat. "What do we do with him?"

"We?" Allat regarded Suramo with a touch of contempt. "I recall you were the one who insisted that a European journalist, particularly a photographer, might be useful. I prefer a man who accepts his own responsibilities when things go wrong." He didn't wait for an answer. "Palu, how long was he in there?"

The withered arm moved uncertainly.

"*Masakan* . . . I do not know."

"But it would be long enough," said Manton in a low, worried voice, his face pale. "Let him out of here and we're finished."

One of the strangers muttered quickly, and his companion scowled. Allat smiled at them and shook his head. "Nothing is changed. There will be no need." Leaning back against the table, he regarded Cord thoughtfully. "But it is true, there have been other things, not all of which I can understand. Perhaps you will help, Mr Cord. Any man can point a camera. But . . ." his voice held a sudden, cutting edge " . . . what else are you?"

"I travel a lot," said Cord mildly.

Allat's lips gave a fractional twist which was part amusement, part impatience. "That much I can believe."

"Djakarta would hardly send a European . . ." Colonel Suramo gnawed his lip unhappily.

"Djakarta?" Allat dismissed the notion. "They would have neither the brains

218

nor the money." He looked at Cord again and shrugged. "Perhaps he is just an inquisitive fool who would like to be a hero. My own feeling is something very different — and we do not even know if he is alone. Yet to squeeze out the truth would take too much time. We have only till tomorrow night."

"So what happens?" demanded Cord, his manner still unruffled. "Another disappearance?"

"He will certainly be missed," reminded Colonel Suramo hastily.

"That? You can tell your other guests he had to leave — a *tilgram* from his employers will be a good enough story." Allat scowled his impatience and gestured to the two watchful strangers. "My friends are here to talk of more important things, and their time is short. Palu . . . "

"Captain?" The man grinned expectantly and came forward.

"You take him and . . . " Allat's voice died away. The others in the room were suddenly staring past him.

Janos Manton, his mouth hanging open, pointed wordlessly. The French windows at the far end of the room had swung open. Peter Dimo stood in the opening, an automatic carbine in his hands, a lopsided grin on his face.

Palu was the only one to act. The Mauser pistol came up — then went flying as Cord swung the camera in his hand like a club, smashing it against the man's wrist. The pistol hit the floor with a clatter and Palu nursed his wrist, cursing.

"You should have let me shoot him," mused Dimo, stepping forward. "*Tidak* . . . no!" The carbine jerked emphatically as one of the strangers began to slide a hand towards his jacket. The hand dropped down again. "Everything will remain very still, because this gun is strange to me and might fire." Conversationally, he added, "It belongs to the little friend you had on watch outside, if it is of interest. Talos . . . "

Cord grinned, reached across the table,

and quickly palmed the Neuhausen. "Nice to see you, Peter."

"I can imagine." Dimo stayed where he was. "Ready to leave?"

"In a moment." Cord ripped the tape reel from the recorder, stuffed it in one pocket, and glanced around. "That's about it, unless we take one of them with us as a sample."

"Wrong time, wrong place. Better walk round the fringe — I want a clear field of fire."

"The tape's only a copy," said Allat hoarsely. "Cord, there are just two of you. Perhaps, if you listen . . . "

"A deal?" Cord gave a soft, dry laugh. "You should know better." He moved back and joined Dimo.

"When we go out, turn left," said Dimo quietly, lips hardly moving. "There's a car parked about forty yards away — probably the one that brought Allat and these two. We make it fast, then try to get past the guardpost at the fence gate. You drive. Okay?"

"Car key?" murmured Cord.

"In the ignition. I took it from the character outside." Dimo raised his voice. "All of you, now — over to the far wall, faces against it, hands on your heads." Sullenly, led by Suramo, they obeyed. He looked at Cord, nodded, and they backed out, moving slowly.

"Now," said Cord softly.

They ran, feet crunching on to gravel as they neared the car, the high-sprung grey sedan he'd seen before. Cord reached the driver's door, flung it open, and heard the first shouts from behind them. As he dived aboard, a gun barked. Dimo had the passenger door open as he key-started the engine. More shots hammered. One spanged off the car's metal and at the same moment he heard Dimo gasp. The young Malaysian half-fell aboard, slamming his door shut as Cord got the car moving, tyres screaming and engine bellowing.

"Remember the gate," gritted Dimo.

"What about you?" Cord forced the wheel round and they took a right turn on to the main driveway.

"Leg — not bad." Dimo glanced back. The firing had stopped, but lights were appearing everywhere and he could see figures running. "What about the gate? We'd better ram it . . ."

Cord shook his head, deliberately switched on the headlights, and, as they swept up towards the closed gate with its tiny guard-post, began a furious series of blasts on his horn.

The sentry hurried out, rifle at the ready, half-blinded by the lights. Cord braked the car to a halt and jumped out.

"*Hai* . . . there's trouble at the house," he shouted, hurrying towards the man. In the background, he could hear the guard post's phone ringing. "Colonel Suramo is hurt. No one to pass — listen, they are calling now."

The guard, confused, lowered his rifle. "What happened, *tuan* . . ."

Cord hit him twice, the first deep in the stomach with his left then, as the man folded, a smash behind the neck with his right. As the sentry fell, rifle clattering, he was already sprinting towards the gate. He swung it open, hearing the phone still ringing and, in the background, the noise of other car engines starting up. Then he was back inside the grey car, meeting a strained grin from Dimo, grating the engine into gear again.

They travelled fast once they'd gained the road, heading inland, away from Barumma, the jungle quickly flanking on either side. Cord glanced in the rearview mirror and caught the flickering glow of pursuing headlights. "How far does this run?" he demanded.

"The road?" Dimo had an already blood-soaked handkerchief pressed against his left leg, inches above the knee. "All the way up into plantation country." He winced as they jarred over a pot-hole, the springs bottoming. "There's a turn-off in about half a mile, a logging track." He looked back. "Provided none of them get close enough to follow our tail lights . . ."

"They won't." Cord took up more accelerator, and the car increased speed on the winding road. "I'd like to know one thing. What's your angle on all this?"

Dimo grimaced. "Might as well tell now, I suppose. Commonwealth Joint Intelligence — Malaysian section. That's why I made so much fuss about not wanting my picture taken. Some old friends might have seen it. How about you?"

"A United Nations outfit. Same line of business."

"U.N.?" The young Malaysian shook his head. "Well, I suppose you people have to get into the act sometimes."

"Sometimes," agreed Cord. "Here's the turn-off — hold on."

He dropped a gear and swung the wheel. The car leaned over hard, then bounced and swayed as it hit the rough logging track. They travelled for about a hundred yards, the jungle dense on either side, then Cord stopped the car, switched off the lights, and got out, the Neuhausen ready. Dimo had the passenger door open, carbine cradled on his lap.

In just under a minute the first car roared past on the main road, headlights filtering momentarily through the thick, screening tapestry of foliage. A little way behind came a second, then a third. As the lights vanished and the sound of engines died away, there was a moment's absolute silence. Then, like some strident bugle-call, a night bird screeched among the trees. Slowly, the jungle's unsleeping life reasserted itself — humming, clicking, squeaking.

"Old tricks are usually the best." Dimo gave a long sigh and relaxed his grip on the carbine. "Now what?"

"We'll have a look at that leg while we've got the chance," said Cord grimly. "Then maybe it'll be easier to decide the rest."

There was a small torch in the car's glove compartment. He had Dimo hold it while he used his clasp-knife to cut a long slit in the blood-soaked trouser leg and inspected the wound. When he looked up, he was considerably relieved. "Clean and shallow — I've done worse shaving. How does it feel?"

"Like I should have nailed that Palu when I had the chance," gritted Dimo. "He was first out back there."

"Be my guest next time." Cord rolled up his own trouser leg, retrieved the taped ammunition magazines, then salvaged the same strips of tape to bind his handkerchief as a fresh padding over the wound. His necktie and a clean duster from the car's glovebox supplemented as an outer bandage. "Try it now." Using the carbine as a support, Dimo got to his feet, took a couple of slow, stiffly cautious steps, and nodded. "I'll manage."

"But you wouldn't break any records." Cord found a cheroot, lit it, and frowned over the glowing tip. "Got any really friendly friends around here?"

"After tonight?" Dimo grimaced ruefully. "I'm not sure. By now Suramo is probably accusing us of every crime

227

that's happened around Barumma in the past decade." He leaned against the car's side, his young, spectacled face suddenly serious. "*Sekarang* . . . well, that's the end of another chapter. I've been monitoring this area for the past couple of years, courtesy of Rajah-Laut. I almost enjoyed it."

"Does Jameson Taggart know what's been going on?"

"No." Dimo chuckled. "Let's just say the Malaysian government has a friend on the company board. It's been good cover — until now."

"Then you had to blow it, because of me." Cord nodded his silent appreciation. "What brought you outside that window?"

"Same reasons as your own, I expect." Dimo fumbled for a cigarette and accepted a light. "We've known for months now something unpleasant was shaping. Indonesia can blow itself sky-high for all I care, but Malaysia's the next-door neighbour — we don't want hurt in the process." He shrugged.

"Suramo couldn't organise anything bigger than a mouse-hunt, and I'd pretty well fixed on Major Karog as our storm-centre. He has ambitions. Only trouble is, almost since the moment you were landed on my lap all my nice, tight theories have been wrecked, one by one."

Something large and loud and hungry bellowed among the trees in the far distance. Cord moved a little closer to the car. "Doorn Allat gets my vote. I'm ready to stake a year's expenses he's the *orang-laut*'s Captain Muka — and that his name isn't Allat. My guess is that's why Chou Sie was kidnapped from the *Tari*. He'd met the real Allat, something none of the other diamond merchants coming here had done."

Dimo showed no particular surprise. "I more or less decided that last night. I saw Allat meet some pretty rough company up-river."

"Then you were the one who got chased?" Cord rubbed a puzzled hand across his chin. "I was there with Kate

Shellon, watching from the other side. But you were back at the hotel . . . "

"When you and the redhead returned?" Dimo drew on his cigarette, grinning. "Well, you must have stopped along the way. Believe me, I didn't." He grew more serious. "How much does she know?"

"Only a little. But you'd better hear the rest." Cord started at the beginning, keeping the story to a tight, factual minimum. Whatever his reactions, Dimo didn't interrupt and his face stayed impassive until the very end.

"And the tape means little Sadiah's involved," he mused at last. "That's a disappointment. But how'd they manage it?"

"Kate had a feeling they were a tape short after the recording session with Pak Gadjal," reminded Cord. "Give a trained expert like Sadiah some dubbing equipment, the kind you'd find in any radio station, and she could alter a tape any way you want."

"But the words . . . " protested Dimo.

"They can build up their own," said Cord harshly. "All they need is a couple of minutes of anyone talking, enough to capture the voice sounding most of the vowels and consonants." He searched for a moment for an example. "Look, suppose they wanted to have someone say my name. They'd simply take a 'k' from some word, 'or' from another, then find a nice 'd' to round it off. Out it would come, Cord — tone, inflection, exactly as it should be. So they juggle words, phrases, sentences around, build words when they need them, and the net result is Pak Gadjal telling the locals to get ready for a shooting war."

"I have heard of this sort of thing, vaguely," murmured Dimo. "The Communists faked some propaganda broadcasts using their prisoners. That was Korea and Vietnam . . . "

"To name only two," agreed Cord. "It's legitimate treatment on regular broadcasting too, when any station wants to tidy up a recording. But what matters is there's got to be some concrete reason for Pak Gadjal being heard. Just what's meant by the dragons roaring . . . " he shook his head.

"There is a gap or two I can fill," said Dimo softly. He dropped his cigarette and stubbed it out with the carbine's butt. "Back there, in the room, there were two strangers. You would see Allat treated them with reasonable respect. He had cause. One of them was Pang Arlac, whose picture is in our Headquarters files. He was a top man in the Huks — you have heard of them?"

Cord whistled softly and nodded. The Hukbo Mapagpalayang Bayan, the self-styled Filipino People's Liberation Army, had been crushed but not destroyed years back. There were still several hard-core groups leading a bandit existence in the Southern Philippines.

"And the other one?"

"I'm not so sure," confessed Dimo. "But my guess would be he's Indonesian PKI Communist brass, from Celebes. One of the *kumpits* up-river last night came from there — I found that much out."

It fitted the cable he'd had from Field Reconnaissance, it fitted his own suppressed fears. Both the Southern Philippines and the great, spider-like crawl of Celebes were within easy sailing range. If men and arms from both places were arriving in Barumma, then Doorn Allat had a ready-made spearhead, regardless of whatever he'd created locally.

"Well, we haven't long to wait to find out, just till tomorrow night," said Dimo gloomily. "What's your guess? A raid on the Kuwa Island diamonds make a good starting point."

"But only a starting point," said Cord, shaking his head. "Peter, suppose there's a Barumma uprising and a phoney declaration of local independence. What could the Djakarta government do about it, and how fast could it spread?"

"With the Tan Sallong legend as marching song?" Dimo treated the idea dolefully. "Ghosts almost forgotten, rising side by side. ... I wouldn't bet which way any of the army units would jump, apart from the few like Colonel Pappang's little honour guard. Indonesia would have a score of uprisings in its eastern sector within a week. Half the islands are simmering with scores to settle. Politics would be secondary."

"How about the Philippines and your own people?"

"The Philippines would have some nasty localised incidents in the south, but could cope. Malaysia ... " a wisp of humour entered his voice " .. internally, we'd be all right. All we've got are a few very tired terrorists growing old gracefully in the northern jungles. They don't harm anyone and it's cheaper to leave them there than have to feed them in jail."

But it still meant that Barumma would be the detonator which could set off an explosion, the kind of explosion which would send blastwaves rippling out over a wide area of the Pacific, cause new bloodshed, create new border tensions, escalate existing confrontations.

Cord sighed. "You wouldn't have a radio link handy?"

"Sorry." Dimo shrugged regretfully. "And I can't suggest we try to get to see Colonel Pappang, even though he has one. By now he'll have heard Suramo's version of the tale and be ready to shoot us on sight."

"We still won't do any good here." Cord thumbed at the car. "Get in."

"Eh?" Dimo blinked. "Everything that wears a uniform will be looking for us!"

"But not where we're going, back into Barumma," Cord sounded more positive than he felt.

"Suppose we meet a roadblock . . ."

"Then you try some of that fast

talking you're so good at, plus this . . . "
Cord handed him the military police
warrant card he'd taken from Karog's
sergeant. "The main problem is avoiding
the main road where it passes district
headquarters. Do that, and we can hide
the car somewhere just outside of town
and walk the rest."

"Well, I never did reckon you as
a photographer," said Dimo in a
dazed voice. "But this — all right,
I think there's another track leading
off this one. If I'm right, we dodge
district headquarters. Then if we reach
Barumma, I've a contact who'll hide
the car and take us in."

"Who?"

Dimo shook his head. "Wait till we
get there," he said firmly. "That way,
if anything goes wrong, what you don't
know you can't tell."

★ ★ ★

Their luck held, but the going was
rough. If the lumber track's surface

236

was poor, the other straggling path was just one degree short of impossible — a disused, overgrown apology corrugated by surface rock, thick tree roots and sudden potholes. In bottom gear, running on sidelights, the swaying car took major punishment. Nursing the clutch, knuckles bone-tight round the steering wheel, Cord winced each time the sump grated against some sharp, unseen protrusion. Indistinct shapes fled high in the foliage, chattering monkeys escaping from this sudden invader.

Somehow, the car survived. A last axle-deep wallow across an abomination of a muddy stream bed and they bounced over a ridge to join tarmac. It was the main road. A scatter of lights in the distance pinpointed Barumma, and the jungle was behind them.

Thankfully, Cord stopped the car and wiped the sweat-soaked palms of his hands down the front of his jerkin. "Where now, Peter?"

"Straight on. You'll pass a couple of

rice paddies, then turn off at a clump of pines. There's a villa set back from the road. Drive round the back." Dimo's voice was forced and miserable. He sat huddled with his wounded leg stretched out, but his real trouble was the way his stomach had reacted to the pitching. He moistened his lips. "I'd appreciate you not trying to break records."

Chuckling through his own fatigue, Cord obeyed. They reached the pine trees after a couple of miles, turned off on to a narrow, gravel-covered service road, and the house was silhouetted ahead. Dimo navigating, the car purred into a large, empty courtyard at the rear. No lights shone in the house, there was no sign their arrival had been noted. He glanced at his watch and, startled, saw it was well after midnight.

"Wait here." Eagerly Dimo opened his door. "I won't be long."

He limped off, disappearing into the dark shadow of the villa and its outhouses. Warily, Cord inspected what he could of the surroundings then at last heard returning footsteps. Dimo came shuffling back, giving a brief, reassuring wave. At his side, a silk dressing gown over pyjamas and slippers, came Hendrik Brink. More amazed than he'd care to admit, Cord slipped out of the car and stared at the slight, elderly Dutchman.

"I'll be damned . . ."

"Not just at this moment, I trust, Mr Cord." Doctor Brink's wrinkled face showed a flicker of amusement, but his voice was clipped and precise. "Though it's true that a considerable number of people would have no objection tonight. Let's go inside — I will see what my first-aid cabinet can provide for your friend's leg."

"The car . . ."

"Will go under cover," said Brink. He saw Cord hesitate, and nodded reassuringly. "I have three native servants, Mr Cord, a couple and their son. The son was born in this house — they are reliable."

239

Five minutes later, Talos Cord was sitting in what seemed the biggest, most comfortable armchair he'd ever known. The cut crystal glass in his right hand contained three fingers of amber malt whisky, his feet rested on a king-sized tigerskin rug. Doctor Brink's study, blinds drawn, only a small table-lamp burning, smelled equally of leather-bound books, tobacco and furniture polish. Outside, a muscular young Dusun had already tucked the grey sedan into Brink's barn-like garage, bringing the doctor's big black Packard out into the open to make room.

Cord wriggled his feet out of their moccasins, took another long sip from the glass, and fought back a yawn. Outside the study, across the hallway, he could hear the soft murmur of Dimo's voice. Doctor Brink was getting the picture, and fast — but Dimo was making sure of the version.

That hardly mattered. What did,

the only thing that did, was what they should do next. He stared down at the tigerskin, not really seeing it, an assorted variety of equally useless totally disconnected possibilities coming to mind one by one and being just as quickly rejected.

The door creaked open and he looked up. Brink entered the room first, his face pinched with worried anger. Dimo was close behind, still limping, wearing a pair of fresh, borrowed slacks in place of his own bloodstained clothing.

"Don't get up," said the Dutchman with grave courtesy. He waved Dimo to a seat, poured two more drinks, then, once they were settled, looked at each of his visitors in turn. The bright blue eyes were strained and bitter. "Peter has told me about your part in all this, Mr Cord."

"All of it," murmured Peter Dimo, leaning back. "Talos, I told you there was only one place we could go. This is it — and Doctor Brink deserves to know. He has — well, helped me before."

"I'm not complaining," said Cord mildly. "But — well, he's still chairman of the Tan Sallong Society."

"I am." Brink nodded wearily, ignoring the glass at his side. "Until tonight, it has been, to my innocent mind, a cultural society — one I supported. One I still support for its original aims." He shrugged. "Perhaps in the circumstances, I seem a fool — but old men look to the past for the lessons needed to shape the future, Mr Cord. Someday you will understand why. I have never had reason to suspect the Society had any purpose beyond genuine cultural activity."

"You're prepared to believe us, though?" asked Cord.

A strangely bitter smile crossed the Dutchman's face. "Of course. After all, in a way, I can claim credit for your being here — is that not so, Peter?"

"He gave me the first tip," said Dimo quietly. "We'd already established an understanding about what I was doing. He got me out of trouble one night, with some very unfriendly characters close behind."

"It was an interesting moment," agreed Brink. The blue eyes flickered back to Cord. "My loyalties are perhaps complex to an outsider, Mr Cord. Let us say that as a magistrate I made my own judgments — it becomes a habit hard to break. I would however, like to see Indonesia grow to adult stature."

"You still help Dimo." Cord said it flatly and deliberately.

"True." The Dutchman smiled, almost sadly. "An adolescent of any kind does not always know best. Until it matures it must sometimes be held in check for its own good." He cleared his throat gently. "That is where your United Nations ideal is slightly faulty. The political adolescents are allowed too strong a voice, too soon."

Cord shrugged. "Nothing's perfect. Even some of our alleged adults can act pretty wild."

"Some other time we will talk about that." Brink pursed his lips. "For now, it is more important that a few months back I heard a strange story from Ruama — the father of the boy who moved your car. He'd been turned back by armed strangers when he tried to visit a relative in one of the up-coast fishing villages, an isolated little place far from anywhere. Perhaps 'turned back' is hardly the word — he ran away. Ruama practises discretion." For the first time, he picked up his drink, tasted it, and added casually, "When I mentioned it to Colonel Suramo he talked of troops in training. I didn't believe him — so I went there with Ruama to find out for myself."

"You took a chance," mused Cord.

"At my age, danger fades. Anyway, when we arrived the strangers had gone — and no one in the village would talk. They had been warned what would happen if they did. However, we — ah — persuaded Ruama's relative. He needed money for a new boat engine.

The villagers had been made to stay in their huts. By night, many boats would come and go. By day there were trucks. Some of the men were soldiers, some were *orang-laut*." The Dutchman swirled the liquor in his glass, his wrinkled face grim. "Mr Cord, during the war I was held in a prison camp. But afterwards we found several Japanese underground supply dumps in this area. There have always been rumours of another, the biggest of all."

"And you think they'd found it!" Cord whistled thinly.

The jungle reclaimed its own quickly, and a lot of years had passed since World War Two. Scattered over the Pacific islands, even some of the known Japanese supply bunkers — rabbit-warren networks was a better description — had never been explored. Their entrances sealed off by explosive charges, they were reminders of a time most people wanted to forget. But, even after so many years, their contents would still, in the main, be as deadly as ever. If Doorn Allat's men — Cord mentally corrected himself, with a moment's wonder about the fate of the real Allat. If Captain Muka's organisation had been able to tap one of these dumps then they would have no lack of arms to distribute to the peasant population they planned to rouse.

"I'd like to hear that tape through in full," said Dimo suddenly. He removed his spectacles and chewed unhappily on one leg of the frame. "Doctor, I don't suppose . . ."

Brink shook his head. "No, I have no recording machine. But this mention of dragons roaring, Mr Cord's suspicions of these *kumpits* he saw off the Isle — part of the key has to be out there."

"We've got to find out, then get the story to Colonel Pappang." Cord rubbed a weary hand across his forehead. "What sort of story did Suramo spread around after we broke out?"

"A good one, from his point of view." The Dutchman shrugged to emphasise the difficulty. "You and Dimo were surprised together while attempting to photograph military documents taken from one of the offices. Major Karog has been ordered to capture you at all costs — and was publicly accused of inefficiency in allowing such a situation to occur. As a result, he has his own score to settle."

"And the girls?" Cord leaned forward, concern twisting across his face to the hairline barrier on his cheek. "How did they react? I'm thinking of Kate — she's left in a hell of a situation."

"Neither said much, neither was questioned." Brink hesitated, then offered his own, reluctant conclusion. "Either Sadiah's part makes them above suspicion or their usefulness as a team is not yet over."

"Could you get a message through to Colonel Pappang?"

"Impossible." Brink shook his head. "First, because by now the causeway

247

to Kuwa will be sealed — and not just because of you. The first of the dancers will be arriving in Barumma by morning, and Pappang will not tolerate them. Second, the only telephone line is a military one. Third, and equally valid, every boat in the harbour will by now be under guard — Major Karog has reason to be particularly efficient."

"All right." Cord accepted the situation, but still saw a chance remaining. "Supposing you were wanting to take Kate and Sadiah — both of them — out to the Isle of Dragons early tomorrow? It would make sense they'd want to see the place in daylight. That way they'd be more prepared for their recordings during the dances. Could you get a boat for that kind of trip?"

Brink thought for a moment, then nodded. "I could. I take it I would have two extra passengers?"

"Only one." Cord grinned, anticipating Dimo's startled protest. "Don't worry, you're going to be busy enough — but with less legwork involved." He swung back to Brink. "Could you manage to get Kate Shellon up here alone, with one of her tape machines, first thing in the morning?"

"I can try," agreed their host. "I will think of some reason."

"Good." Cord had one last question remaining. "There's a man called Palu at the Tengah Imports yard. Know anything about the place?"

"The firm is new and Palu is their local manager." The older man's voice held a new, bitter anger. "He boasts that his arm was shattered in battle during what the Indonesians call their War of Independence." His thin hands gripped tight on the whisky glass. "I have a longer memory. He was employed by the Japanese as a camp guard — we called him the Butcher."

"And the arm?" asked Dimo quietly.

Brink shook his head. "Those of us left were finally transferred to build a road. I heard a story later, that the Butcher had been killed in an

Australian commando raid. I hoped it was true."

"I nearly shot him tonight," mused Dimo.

"The camp was near here?" asked Cord.

Brink nodded. "Inland, Mr Cord."

"Then that's how they know about the Jap supply dump." Cord glanced at Dimo. "Next time, I won't stop you."

Slowly, Brink got to his feet. "For now, I have a suggestion of my own. Get some sleep, my friends. Tomorrow — well, it will be a long day."

Cord knew he was right.

7

THE worst nightmares are those which linger as vague, shapeless horror in the moments of waking. They were the kind Cord had known and accepted since a child, the kind which left him strangely ready for reality, whatever its perils — as long as it was the creation of mere flesh and blood.

The horror was there that morning. But the gentle shake at his shoulder wakened him with only a moment's transition, his fingers already brushing under the pillow, closing on the hard, familiar shape of the Neuhausen's butt.

"You snore like an over-fed cat!"

Dimo's chuckle brought him round, blinking at the bright daylight streaming in through the skylight window above his head. Brink had fixed up two camp-beds in the villa's loft, apologising for the spiders. Cord couldn't remember much after that. He yawned, rubbed his eyes and saw the time on his watch with some surprise.

"After nine," agreed Dimo. "Doctor Brink keeps stricter hours — he's already on his way into Barumma. And the only hostile force in sight is his housekeeper — keeping a late breakfast for you is playing hell with her routine."

Cord levered up on his elbows. "How's the leg?"

"An interesting limp, but I'm mobile." Dimo demonstrated with a few shuffling steps. He was fully dressed, his camp-bed already folded. "While you snored, we had visitors — a jeep-load of Karog's security men. They came to warn old Brink that we might have doubled back." He grinned. "He invited them to have coffee, but they were in too big a hurry."

"And you let me sleep . . ."

"There were only four of them," retorted Dimo airily. Without waiting

252

to argue, he disappeared back down the loft's ladder.

Cord dressed, went down, and found hot water and shaving tackle already waiting for him in the white tiled bathroom. When he finished and walked through to the big, airy dining room, face still smarting, Dimo was lounging back in a chair, smoking. The young Malaysian looked utterly relaxed — but the carbine lay beside him.

Doctor Brink's housekeeper, a fat, grey-haired woman whose feet were bare, came into the room a moment later carrying a tray. She laid it on a table, regarding them with something close to a scowl, and went out again as silently as she'd come.

"We're not popular," sighed Dimo. "Seems she doesn't like to see her boss getting involved in things. But she makes darned good coffee."

With the coffee was buttered toast and boiled eggs. Cord was still sipping the last of the coffee when the sound of an approaching car sent Dimo limping across to the window. He stared out then turned and nodded happily.

"He's back — and it looks like Kate Shellon's with him."

They came into the house a moment later, Kate eagerly in the lead, Brink a tactful pace or two behind. Cord met them in the hallway.

"Talos!" The redhead came straight towards him. Cord smiled at the relief in her eyes, put an arm round her shoulders, and glanced at Brink. "Any trouble?"

"None." Brink patted the lid of the tape machine he was carrying.

"Not like last night." Kate's mouth tightened at the memory. "When I heard the shooting . . ."

"Peter got a scratch, but that was all," Cord reassured her.

"Constant sympathy," complained Dimo, coming towards them. "I might have bled to death."

"What about you, Kate?" Cord kept his grip round the redhead's shoulders and eyed her seriously. "Anyone been asking awkward questions?"

"Only Sadiah." She gnawed her lip and looked down at her shirt and slacks. "Doctor Brink explained why on the way over. It — well, I still can't believe it."

"Which is part of why I want that machine." Cord turned to the older man. "How'd you manage it?"

"We were lucky. Sadiah had another appointment at the radio station, and I suggested Miss Shellon should come with me and see some of the old court records I have here. But the rest is as I thought, soldiers everywhere, everyone entering or leaving the town being checked — though their job is complicated by the first of the villagers arriving for the dances."

"And the boat?"

Brink gave a whimsical nod. "It is arranged — a little later than I would wish, but Major Karog was slightly difficult."

"Karog . . ." Dimo gave a soft whistle. "You saw him?"

"It seemed the best way," said Brink almost apologetically. "I was suitably sympathetic towards his problems. There will be a launch available at noon. I — ah — said it would be pleasant for the ladies to have a picnic lunch with me on the island."

"Then we're in business," said Cord with a thin chuckle of satisfaction. "Kate, let's get that machine of yours ready."

They went through to the study. The redhead took the reel of recording tape from Cord, fed it through the sound head, and glanced up. As the others clustered round, Cord nodded. She pressed a switch key and the reel began to turn.

It took exactly five minutes to play. As the last words faded and the remainder of the tape whirred silently, Cord leaned forward and switched off, his face an unemotional mask. Beside him, Dimo concentrated on lighting a cigarette while Doctor Brink frowned at the floor, lips moving silently, as if still refusing to believe what he'd heard.

The taped voice, only the slightest flaw now and again to indicate how it had been prepared, had talked of "this vile bloodshed", of an act of "foul brutality", a promise of "immediate revenge" — but never, in explicit terms, was the exact reason mentioned. It was a people being called to take up arms, with the promise of support. But arms against what, support from where?

Cord rubbed a hand slowly across his chin. "Kate?"

She shook her head, crossed to the nearest chair and sat down. Her face was pale, her voice little more than a whisper. "It's — it's horrible. Why would she do it?"

"Do reasons matter?" asked Brink quietly. "Perhaps, from her viewpoint, it is the result that counts." He walked over to the window, looked out, and when he turned again, his face was older, greyer than it had ever seemed before. "Mr Cord, I will make a guess. Tonight, when the Dragon Dances are at their height, there will be some tragedy — a tragedy which will be blamed on Pappang and his Javanese soldiers. It will be the signal for general uprising — and if that message, in Pak Gadjal's voice, is heard often enough and the tragedy is sufficiently horrifying then every village in this district will be in a state of armed rebellion within a matter of hours."

"That's how it looks," said Cord simply. "That's why I've got to get back out to the island."

"With Sadiah along for company?" Peter Dimo adjusted his spectacles with an outraged snort. "It doesn't make sense!"

"I want her there." The intensity on Cord's hard, still youthful face was of the kind which tolerates no argument. "I'm going to find out what's there, and then she's going to talk."

"Can you make her?" asked Kate Shellon unsteadily. "Supposing . . ."

He cut her short. "She'll talk, Kate. One way or another. Whatever happens.

You understand why, don't you?"

She looked away from him, scuffing one shoe slowly across the floor, not wanting to answer.

* * *

Kate left the house an hour later to return to Barumma, travelling in the back of Brink's black Packard. The servant Ruama was at the wheel, Peter Dimo up front beside him — the young Malaysian wearing a loose shirt and pantaloons belonging to Ruama's son, a Dusun headcloth wrapped around his head, spectacles in one pocket.

"They should have no trouble," mused the Dutchman, watching the car drive off.

Cord nodded. If there was, Dimo still had the military police warrant card. Once in Barumma, his tasks came down to little more than some dedicated, gossiping inquiries of the type he did so well. As the car disappeared, Cord concentrated on his own problems. After the island, what next? Try to persuade Colonel Pappang that his fellow-colonel was about to attack? Even if Pappang would listen, had he sufficient strength to withstand the Huk and PKI?

What was needed was action in Barumma itself. Peter Dimo would gather part of the information needed for that. And the rest . . .

Suddenly, it came to him. He laughed aloud, a rich chuckle which brought Doctor Brink in immediate, anxious concern. He grinned at the old Dutchman, but shook his head. It was the kind of thing which would have to be worked out carefully.

They were ready and waiting when, about forty minutes later, the Packard returned from Barumma. Ruama was blandly reassuring — there had been no trouble at the road block, the red-haired *wanita* had been delivered to her hotel, Dimo had slipped off earlier, heading up an alleyway at an energetic limp.

Cord took a last look in the hall mirror and grimaced. Like Dimo, he had changed into a loose native shirt and pantaloons, and with his black hair and deeply tanned skin he should escape casual notice. But in any closer inspection his European facial bones would be an immediate give-away. He checked the gun in the right-hand pocket of the pantaloons, adjusted a black Muslim cap on his head, and followed Brink out to the car.

They made the journey in silence, the Packard purring along the dusty road at a leisurely pace, their driver slowing now and again as they overtook parties of villagers — some walking, some riding on ox-carts, a few crammed perilously aboard antiquated trucks.

"On their way in for the Dragon Dances," said Brink quietly. He nodded to one group, laden with cloth-wrapped bundles. "They keep their ceremonial costumes safe until the last minute — most of them have been handed down generation after generation."

"How many will be on the island tonight?" asked Cord.

Brink shrugged. "Dancers? Maybe a couple of hundred — and ten times as many watching. Around here a village is really a family, and the Dragon Dances are a family affair."

The road block was on the outskirts of town. Brink leaned forward, murmured to Ruama, and the native brought the car to a halt with its front wheels some twenty yards short of the barbed wire barrier. The old Dutchman clambered out and went briskly towards the quartet of soldiers on guard. Cord leaned well back, feeling the sweat beading on his forehead, every second dragging out while he watched Brink talk and laugh with the men. At last, the Dutchman gestured towards the car and, whatever he said, it brought fresh laughter. Two of the soldiers dragged the wire trestle clear.

Unhurriedly, Brink strolled back to the Packard, climbed aboard, and shut the door. He nodded to Ruama and the car nosed forward. Cord stayed well back, his head bowed, then they were through, gathering speed.

"Nice going." He moistened his suddenly dry lips. "How'd you explain me away?"

"I said you were a friend." A slight edge of regret entered the man's voice. "People around here take my word for most things. And I knew one of these men — I sent him to jail a couple of times when he was younger, so we are old acquaintances." He leaned forward. "The harbour, Ruama — you know what to do."

Inside town, the narrow streets were crowded with wandering, holiday-mood villagers, wheeled traffic moving through at a crawl amid a constant blast of horns. Here and there, a brightly gay costume with ornate, horned head-dress and bold, heavily beaded waistcloth marked some Dragon Dancer who couldn't restrain his exuberance till evening.

The approach to the harbour was

blocked by another trestle barrier, but Brink got out and spoke briefly to the sergeant in charge. Major Karog's name was an immediate passport. With a smart salute the trestle was moved and the Packard waved through.

"Here, Ruama." Brink signalled the car to halt again a little way down the pier and glanced at Cord. "We walk the rest. And remember, the man on the launch is a friend — he is not to be involved."

Cord followed him out. The Dutchman set a slow, deliberate pace along the heavy wooden planking, refusing to hurry, his keen blue eyes missing nothing.

"More boats than usual," he murmured. "But they come to act as ferries for tonight."

"The ones we're interested in will be hiding up-river, or in creeks along the coast," said Cord grimly. "They wouldn't risk here, not in daylight."

They stopped beside a small, white painted cabin launch. Brink clambered down first then, as Cord joined him on deck, greeted the man who emerged from the tiny wheelhouse. The seaman wore singlet and shorts, was small, dark and relatively toothless, and greeted Brink with grinning gums. Brink talked to him briefly, the grin changed to a slight frown, but at last the thin shoulders shrugged.

"Well?" asked Cord.

"He will not ask questions." Brink pursed his lips. "I suggest you get below now, into the chain locker, and stay there. They should be here soon."

The cabin was small, with an odour of stale bilge-water. Cord opened the tiny, cupboard-like door for'ard and squeezed his way into the cramped confines of the chain locker then, the door pulled shut, crouched in the darkness and waited.

At last, the faint sound of voices was followed by quick footsteps on deck. Moments later, he heard the two girls come into the cabin with Brink. They went out again, the launch engine fired and its mooring lines thudded on deck. They were under way.

Cord stayed where he was, easing from one muscle-aching position to another, feeling the gathering roll as the launch met open sea. At last, as the roll became a steady, rhythmic pitch and spray pattered against the hull, he opened the door and eased his way out. Through one of the cabin's small ports he saw they were already halfway along the length of Kuwa, well out from shore.

Quietly, he climbed the few steps to the launch's wheelhouse. The seaman looked at him, but said nothing. Kate and Sadiah were standing near the stern with Doctor Brink, looking out towards the diamond island.

Cord moved towards them.

"Hello, Sadiah."

The girl spun round. Like Kate, she was in shirt and slacks, with ankle-laced jungle boots. Her round, pert face registered angry surprise and narrow-eyed suspicion in quick succession.

"You!" She glanced quickly at Kate and Brink, to find them watching her in unemotional silence. "*Begitu* . . . so it is like that! You knew he was aboard."

"Does it matter?" asked Cord softly. He padded nearer across the gently rolling deck. "You can guess why, though — can't you?"

She tossed her head stubbornly. "All I know is that you are *perampok* . . . a criminal, wanted by the authorities. Kate, if you and Doctor Brink do not wish to be in similar trouble . . . " she broke off, grabbing a side rail as the launch gave a sudden pitch and a fine curtain of spindrift swept aboard.

"Trouble?" Kate Shellon's voice was strained and acid. "What about what's happened already? I don't like being used as a convenient travelling idiot, the kind of idiot who gave you an excuse for that Pak Gadjal interview."

Cord saw the protest gathering on the other girl's lips and cut her short. "Let's not waste time, Sadiah. You've heard from your friends by now that I got a copy of what you did to that extra tape."

"And we've heard the result," growled Doctor Brink. "Girl, what devilment is behind it? What happens tonight?"

She faced them coolly, the light wind plucking at the collar of her shirt. "Doctor, it need not concern you, affect you in any way. But if you side with Cord and his friend you will be hunted like them."

"With the Huks and the PKI leading the pack?" Cord gave a savage, twisted grin. "A fine bunch of freedom fighters. And what kind of labels do you give to a bought man like Suramo or a butcher like your alleged Allat?" He shook his head in disgust. "No wonder you stayed calm when he boarded the *Tari* as Captain Muka. You knew they only wanted Chou Sie, that they wouldn't harm you, whatever happened. And when he whispered to you, what was it — just a friendly hello, or a message that everything was fine?"

She bit hard on her lip and glanced towards the Indonesian at the helm. He kept his back towards them, deliberately ignoring what he'd decided didn't concern him.

"No help there," said Cord grimly. "He's just a man sailing a boat — and there's a gun in my pocket if anyone did manage to persuade him to change his mind."

Reluctantly, she looked away, out across the water towards Kuwa. "Where are we going?" she asked woodenly.

"To the Isle of Dragons, just like you were promised." Cord reached out, took her chin firmly between finger and thumb, and forced her to meet his gaze. "Only the reason is going to be different — I need answers, Sadiah, and I'm going to get them, either from the island or from you."

She tried to bite his hand, sharp, white teeth snapping on empty air as he jerked back.

He grimaced and glanced at Kate Shellon. "If you look around, maybe you'll find a spare length of rope or something that would do the same job. Then we wouldn't have to worry quite so much about the local wild life."

The redhead nodded. She went into the wheelhouse, returned with a short length of plastic covered wiring flex, and started to secure Sadiah's hands behind her back. The younger girl spat viciously, then gasped as Kate slapped her hard across the face.

"Behave," said Kate brusquely. "Otherwise I'll ram a gag in your mouth. And it'll be the dirtiest chunk of waste rag I can lay my hands on!"

The warning was enough.

★ ★ ★

They brought the white cabin launch in towards the Isle of Dragons, close to the spot where the two *kumpits* had unloaded the previous day. Engine ticking over, the boat gently grounded on the fine, sandy bottom about ten

270

yards from shore. Cord jumped into the warm, knee-high water and offered, "Wade or carry, Sadiah — which?"

Tight-lipped, she let him carry her to the edge of the lapping crystal-clear water while Brink splashed ashore beside them. Cord went back, returned with Kate Shellon, set her down, then looked around. The beach lay empty and deserted, the light wind barely rustling the salt-stunted scrub which began a few feet above high-water mark. A few noisy, high-flying seabirds flapped overhead.

"We should have the place to ourselves," declared Brink. He sniffed the air appreciatively, then qualified his words. "Still, I would be prepared for — ah — the unexpected. Now, where do we start?"

"The ceremonial area," said Cord, untying Sadiah's wrists.

"All I want right now is a straightforward guided tour."

The Dutchman nodded and led the way. Kate went next, Cord and Sadiah bringing up the rear. Small, bright-backed beetles scurried from their path as they left the beach behind, the scrub becoming thick but still patchy, the soil soft and sandy with only an occasional patch of coarse, pebbled shingle.

About two hundred yards on, they reached a well-worn footpath, which was quickly crossed by another. Brink pointed ahead, to a tall, isolated clump of palm trees.

"That's the place — you can see where the fires have been made ready."

Automatically, their pace quickened. Even Sadiah looked around with a sudden return of interest. To one side of the palms, ringed by scrub and tough, tufted grass, a natural bowl-like depression had been smoothed flat and bare by generations of use. About three hundred yards in diameter, the sandy, hard-packed dance arena was bounded by four high bonfire stacks of driftwood and other inflammable debris, spaced round its edge with precise care. Beneath the palm trees, dumped with considerably less precision, lay a quantity of metal drums and casks.

"Kerosene for the pressure lamps they'll string around the bowl and water for drinking," explained Brink as they moved nearer. "There's no fresh water on the island."

Cord checked the first of the casks, rocking it until he heard the splash of liquid. The kerosene drums seemed equally genuine. He stood back, wiping the perspiration from his forehead with a shirt-sleeve.

"Let's see if I've got it right. The main festival is held here, dancers in the arena, bonfires going, spectators all around. Then what?"

"The procession." Brink pointed to the far side of the bowl. "Through that gap in the bushes — there's another path down to the beach, on the other side of the island. That's where they used to stake out the sacrifices. The procession goes down, then some token offerings are left on the beach. After

273

that they come back here and take up where they left off."

Frowning, Kate Shellon leaned against one of the water casks. "Talos, just what are we looking for anyway?"

"Ask her," shrugged Cord, jerking his head towards Sadiah, standing scowling a few feet away. "She knows better than I do." He sighed and beckoned them on again. "Let's cover the rest of it."

Kicking a loose pebble ahead of him, he led the way across the dance bowl. Once or twice he glanced at the silent, fringing scrub, uneasily conscious of the way they were exposed, a marksman's dream. The sun, high overhead, seemed to shimmer its glare in waves across the baked, sandy floor.

Suddenly, he stopped — so suddenly that Kate almost collided with him. Narrowing his eyes, Cord was still uncertain whether it might be mere imagination or a trick of light which made one of the ripples seem steady and constant in colour and substance.

"Anything wrong?" Puffing a little,

Brink regarded him querulously.

"I'm not sure. Give me a minute." He left them and walked towards the spot. The sandy soil seemed as level as the rest, but — yes, he was right. Faintly different in shade from the rest of the bowl, a thin, inches wide line ran arrow-straight from the scrub's edge right into the centre. And at the centre . . .

The same slightly darker stain, but this time as long and wide as a truck.

The world seemed to shrink until all that remained was that line and its pendulum-like ending. Cord dropped to his knees, fingers scrabbling in dog-like fashion. The sandy soil melted away, and he stared, fascinated, at the thin, double-core wire he'd uncovered. He looked back. The others were still standing where he'd left them.

Running now, he made for the centre of the arena, then pawed again with a frantic urgency.

Once more the smooth, level surface was a mere veneer over loose, disturbed sand. It had been dug, and recently. It had been smoothed and levelled with elaborate care. But the greatest care in the world couldn't have obliterated that faint difference in coloration, the difference between long exposed surface grains and what had lain beneath.

Rapid, light footsteps brought his head up. Kate was hurrying towards him, Brink close behind — the Dutchman gripping Sadiah by the arm, dragging her with him.

"Found something?" asked the red-head eagerly as she drew near.

Cord nodded and pointed towards the nearest of the stacked beacons. "Get me a flat piece of wood, anything I can use on this." As he spoke, he resumed digging into the loose, sandy soil.

By the time she'd returned with two yard-long sections of broken deck planking, Brink and Sadiah had arrived and were standing watching, puzzled and silent.

"Right." He grabbed one of the

lengths of wood and began shovelling. Brink hesitated uncertainly then took the other makeshift spade and joined him.

The hole was two feet deep when Cord's piece of planking suddenly hit something hard and unyielding. He waved Brink aside and used his hands to clear away the last layer of covering sand.

The wooden ammunition box had once been painted yellow. The paint was cracked and faded, the black, stencilled lettering partly worn away by time. But the lettering was Japanese, and the edge of another box was plainly visible.

Beside him, Brink was cursing in a low, horrified voice. The two girls were motionless, still uncertain. His lips a hard, tight line, Cord gripped the edge of the first box and forced it up on its end. Underneath was another layer. Wordlessly, Brink had started shovelling again. There were more boxes all around, the sizes and shapes varying. One had a loose lid, and Cord wrenched it open. Glistening in their thin skin of protective factory grease, exactly as they must have left some Japanese munitions plant long years before, row upon row of percussion grenades met the sun's glare.

"Try another." The words came from Brink in a hoarse, forced whisper.

He took the nearest. The lid was harder to move, and a long splinter of wood tore a gash in one finger as he levered the box open. Inside nestled a score of mortar bombs. Slowly, Cord looked up.

"They said the dragons would roar, Sadiah. And now we know why." The same, distilled fury in his voice, he strode towards her. "Like to imagine what will happen when that stuff goes up — goes up when this place is full of people, laughing people, happy people?"

She shrank back from him, trying to shake her head, strange, protesting noises trying to come from her throat.

Suddenly, Kate stepped between them and gripped the girl by the arm.

"Sadiah, didn't you know?"

She swallowed hard and tried again, her eyes staring past them towards the opened boxes. "*Tidak* . . . no, never! That there would be an explosion, a diversion, perhaps panic, yes — but not this. They didn't say . . . " her voice broke and she closed her eyes tight, trying to shut out the terrible reality in front of her.

"I — I'll believe that." Quietly, Kate let her go and turned to Cord. "How much damage would it do?"

He shook his head. "Depends how much more is buried and the condition it's in. But my guess is there's enough to blow half the island skyhigh."

"And anyone in the dance arena along with it," agreed Brink bitterly, sitting on the edge of the hole, his mouth twisted. "It would be a giant land-mine — blast, shrapnel, and chaos. This would start your revolution, Cord — start it in a way which would sweep the land."

"With Pak Gadjal's little speech to do the rest." Cord nodded and looked again at the trembling girl. "What's the rest, Sadiah? Were they planning for you and Kate to be out on the fringe, so that you could come back and tell all about it — like they'd thought of having a certain photographer along, with a bonus of tragedy to film?"

She didn't answer. He shrugged at Kate. "Keep an eye on her Doctor, maybe you'd like to see what else there is around. I've got the line of the detonator wiring, and I want to see where the other end leads."

Kate laid an urgent, restraining hand on his arm. "If they left someone to guard the firing end . . . "

Cord shrugged. "Ask Sadiah."

The other girl shook her head, her whole manner still dull and shaken. "I — I don't know."

"If they did, then he'd have seen us by now and could have done something about it," said Cord more crisply than he felt. Until they'd found the cache of explosives they'd been safe enough, but now things were different. He smiled encouragingly. "Just stay close to here. This won't take long."

The walk back across the flat, empty bowl of the arena, following the thin, almost invisible line which marked the buried wire, seemed very long and very lonely. By the time he reached the start of the scrub his mouth was dry and his stomach tight with tension. But still nothing happened. Cord glanced back. The others were still where he'd left them, and Brink was digging again.

Once in the scrub, the wire's path hadn't been hidden with quite so much care. It snaked between individual bushes, following the easiest route, once even surfaced for a few inches to cross a narrow outcrop of rock. Then, suddenly, roughly two hundred yards from the dance arena's edge, he found its end. The double-core cable popped up, wires already bared and twisted, waiting to be dropped on the terminals of the firing battery.

The Neuhausen ready, he checked around with an even finer care. The signs were plain enough — footprints, cigarette stubs, a piece of leafy, broken branch which someone might have used as a fly-whisk. A tiny wisp of smoke rose from nearby. A cigarette end, still smouldering. Beside it, two distinct sets of footprints in the soft soil led away, deeper into the scrub. It took a moment to realise why. Then he swore aloud and started to run, heading for the launch, throwing caution aside for urgency, knowing why the watchers hadn't stopped them when the digging began. Long thorns clawed at his legs and body as he ran, heedless of anything except the most direct path. Twice he stumbled and almost fell as some gnarled root caught at his feet.

The blue of the sea glinted ahead, and he reached the last fringe of scrub. Cord slowed, sighing thankfully as he saw the launch was still where they'd left it, the waves nudging against her hull then rippling on over the shallows towards the shore. But something else was lying there, half in, half out of the water, being tugged at gently by the ebb and flow. Keeping to the scrub's fringe, he went nearer — already certain of what he'd find.

The launch's Indonesian crewman lay face down, one hand stretched out on the dry sand in claw-like fashion, head twisted obscenely to one side, eyes staring blank and lifeless.

It was a sufficient trademark without having to go nearer. Cord froze where he was, thinking fast. He'd had one sharp lesson already that he was up against professionals, pure luck had brought him to the beach at a point lower down than where the launch lay. If they were using the crewman's body as bait, waiting to have him step into the open . . . a thin, humourless grin touched his mouth and he quietly edged back into the thick scrub, crouching low, his senses in a new sharp focus, almost welcome in its simplicity. No borderline issues here, no restraints or doubts. This was a hunt . . . but the hunted was turned hunter.

What he'd hoped for happened a couple of minutes later. A rustle was carried by the faint wind, a bush shivered unnaturally as the man patiently hiding behind it shifted into a more comfortable position. Cord began crawling, ignoring the undergrowth which brushed his face, the insects which fell on to his clothing, forcing himself to breathe slowly and regularly, knowing that to hurry would be fatal.

At last, he was ready. The bush was about ten yards away and now a little behind him, on the left. It had to happen now. He rose gradually, saw the man crouching by the bush, glimpsed the glint of blued metal in his hand — and then had been seen in turn.

It was the one-armed Palu's smaller companion. The dark face showed startled surprise, the figure twisted frantically, gun arm swinging — then Cord shot him twice, aiming for the chest, the reports blending almost as one. As the man jerked to full height and started to fall sheer reflex action sent Cord diving to one side, rolling as he hit the ground, hearing the harsh, rapid snapping of another gun while bullets plucked vigorously at the scrub above his head.

As suddenly as it had begun, the firing stopped. But Palu was out there, watching, waiting, listening. Probably over on the right, guessed Cord. And now each could wait for the other to make the next move — wait or take the initiative, take a chance. Thoughtfully, he considered the Neuhausen. Like most of its kind, the automatic held a seven-shot clip.

He'd fired twice. And Palu was a professional.

Mind made up, he took one of the spare clips from his pocket, extracted the partly used magazine, fed the fresh one in its place, then groped around and gathered a handful of medium-sized pebbles. Lying flat, gun arm extended, he began triggering. Five shots snarled from the Neuhausen, the bullets searching a thirty degree arc through the area of scrub where Palu had to be. As the last shot died, Cord tossed the pebbles over his shoulder. They crashed their way through the scrub and pattered to earth, the sound that might be made by a man making a sudden retreat.

He lay very still.

At first, there was nothing — only the rank odour of cordite and hot gun-oil in the air, the murmur of the sea in the background. Then there was a slow, gentle ripple in the bushes. It stopped for a moment, resumed, stopped again, and suddenly Palu was visible, a head and shoulders coming nearer, a coarse, ugly face with the lips drawn back from clenched teeth, eyes which glittered with a killing lust.

Slowly, carefully, Cord took up the tension of the Neuhausen's trigger. His mouth puckered, he ran his tongue over dry lips, and gave a sharp whistle. Palu's head swung round and the Neuhausen fired. As the automatic kicked in Cord's hand a round hole blossomed between Palu's eyes. The man's mouth fell open, all expression wiped from his face. He took another half-step then pitched forward, dead before he hit the ground.

★ ★ ★

When, at last, Cord returned to the Dragon Dance bowl he found the scene prepared for battle. The hole in the middle had been deepened, the lip ringed with ammunition boxes, and its three occupants were barely visible behind their improvised shelter.

Kate was first to come scrambling out, her face still pale beneath the freckled tan, her eyes spelling out the tension she'd lived through in the short time he'd been gone.

"It's over," he told her. "For now,

anyway." He glanced past her at the other two. Something else had happened while he'd been away, and not just the fact that Sadiah Beh had one of the Japanese grenades held awkwardly in her right hand. "Sadiah, whatever you were going to do with that thing, you'd better put it down."

She obeyed more than willingly. "It was the *dokter* — he said we should be ready in case you did not come back."

Sheepishly, Brink nodded. "When we heard the shooting they wanted to go to you. I made them stay."

"It was the best idea, either way." Cord's mouth tightened at the memory of what he'd left, then he smiled. "Nice little fort you've got. I wonder, though . . . " he nudged the nearest of the ammunition crates with one foot. "The stuff inside these can get temperamental with age. A bullet through the wrong case and you wouldn't have had time to worry about what happened next."

"That's what I thought," confessed Kate wryly. "But there didn't seem much point in arguing."

"And the shooting?" asked Brink.

"There were two of them, and they got to the launch first. We'll have to take it back on our own." As the others fell silent, Cord switched his interest back to Sadiah. "Looks like you made a conversion while I was gone."

"These crates made it for us," declared Kate almost protectively. "I'm willing to believe her."

"Circumstances bring their own reactions," nodded Brink with a heavy, sombre formality. His shirt and jacket were dark with sweat, his hands and face were caked with grit, but Cord could suddenly picture the Dutchman as he must have been in his judicial prime, ruling his court of law. "I would not excuse this child completely. I think . . . " he shrugged a little " . . . I think perhaps she will create her own punishment now that there is realisation. For the rest — I think you should hear her story."

"Sadiah?" Cord raised a questioning eyebrow.

She bit her lip. "When you are at school, a student, what should be done, what should be right, seems simple and neat and tidy . . ."

"And easy," agreed Cord softly. "I thought that once myself. Everybody does."

"I — I know when the signal is to be given," she volunteered.

"When?"

"Ten o'clock tonight. When the dances are at their peak, just before the procession."

"Good." He'd known already. It had been carefully printed on a sheet of paper he'd found in Palu's pocket when he searched the two men before dragging their bodies a little way into the scrub. He'd been more gentle in bringing the dead seaman out of reach of the water. "The next job is to fill in this hole again, leave things as they were."

Brink groaned. "Why?"

"Because the dances have to go ahead," he explained patiently. "Soon as we're finished, we get back to Barumma. We pick up Peter Dimo." He hesitated, then took the one remaining gamble. "Sadiah, you were to report to Allat when you returned?"

She nodded.

"Then do it. Say everything went smoothly. Act as naturally as you can, then get out to Doctor Brink's place. Peter and I will be there with him."

"And me?" queried Kate. "Are you leaving me out?"

"No." His eyes twinkled. "You've a job too. Give us about an hour, then find Major Karog, tell him Doctor Brink wants to see him urgently and alone — and come out with him." He scrubbed a hand across his chin, amused at their incredulous reaction. "We're about to enlist the major, whether he likes it or not."

8

THE white cabin launch attracted little attention as it came back alongside the pier at Barumma. They tied up, left the boat, and walked to where the black Packard and its driver still waited. Doctor Brink trailed behind a little, a cloth-wrapped bundle cradled stubbornly in his arms despite Cord's offer to help. Bringing back one of the mortar bombs had been his idea, and he was going to stay responsible for it.

Once again, the car was waved through the harbour barrier without formality. Beyond it, if Barumma had seemed busy before it now appeared ready to burst at the seams. Food stalls were doing a roaring trade at every corner of the clogged, noisy streets. The sound of cymbals and drums rang loud. Barumma was en-fête.

Kate and Sadiah left them near the Harimau, and the Packard nosed slowly through the crowds again, the congestion gradually thinning as they reached the fringe of town. Peter Dimo was waiting where they'd arranged, lounging in the shade of a tree near the road's verge. He grinned as the car drew up, tossed away a half-smoked cigarette, and limped over.

"You're late." He clambered aboard and dropped into the rear seat. "Late — and I'm hungry."

"We had problems," said Cord dryly. "What's the road-block situation?"

"Still checking incoming traffic, not bothering about anything leaving town." Dimo yawned. "The rest is as you guessed. The Tengah yard is bulging with men, Allat's staying close to the other diamond buyers, and most of Suramo's soldier-boys are being kept well out of town. Oh, and if you're interested, we're now worth 50,000 rupiahs each on delivery — no quibbles about condition on receipt."

"Then we should remove possible temptation," murmured Brink. He nodded to Ruama and the car started moving. Two minutes later they'd been waved through the roadblock, the men on duty too busy with incoming villagers to do more than glance at the Packard as it passed.

"Now, how'd you make out?" demanded Dimo as the car gathered speed along the dusty road.

They told him, and his face lost its humour. He lit a fresh cigarette with a slow and thoughtful care.

"Can you trust Sadiah?"

"We haven't much option." Cord put it bluntly. "If she tells Allat everything's fine we're in business. But if she hadn't shown up as arranged he'd have guessed there was trouble. Every move we make right now is a gamble."

"I would trust her," said Doctor Brink, his voice quietly positive. He watched the road unwind ahead for a moment. "She told me quite a

294

lot about herself on the way back — she wanted to talk to someone about it. On Celebes, her family are reasonably wealthy. So they sent her to Manila to be educated — a wise step, except that she listened to the wrong people, accepted the wrong things." The Dutchman smiled almost sadly, with his own memories. "When I was a student back home, it was quite fashionable to be an anarchist."

Dimo shrugged and without further comment relaxed into a sleepy-eyed silence.

★ ★ ★

Whatever the circumstances, Doctor Brink's household ran smoothly. Lunch was on the table when they arrived — cold cuts with a fresh, crisp salad with steaming black coffee to wash it down. They ate with one eye on the road leading to the house and, as they finished, Sadiah drove up in the jeep the girls had been loaned. She parked it, got out, and walked quickly towards the house.

Cord greeted her arrival in deliberately friendly fashion, then asked, "You saw Allat?"

"*Ja*. I told him all had gone smoothly." She took a deep breath and looked hopefully towards Brink. "Doing that will — will help against the rest?"

"A great deal," he assured her, then smiled a little. "And you have earned yourself something to eat."

"It's ready and waiting." Peter Dimo beckoned from the serving table, a filled plate in one hand. "Sadiah, I want someone to talk to — and I like an appreciative, good-looking audience."

Her eyes thanked him and she went over. But, watching the girl eat while Dimo chattered — chattering which every now and then included a sudden, shrewd question — Cord guessed it would be a long time before Sadiah recovered her previous confident liveliness. For now at any rate she was suffering from a blend of shock and guilt, from the collapse of the hazy, heroic role she'd created for herself.

Time passed. He had smoked his way through two cheroots and was arguing with himself about lighting another when Brink, keeping watch by the window, narrowed his eyes then gave a grunt of warning.

"Karog's station wagon . . . ."

"On its own?" Cord scrambled over. The green station wagon coming towards the house was the only vehicle in sight. As it drew nearer, he counted three people aboard — a driver up front, two passengers at the rear.

They'd rehearsed what to do. While Brink went to meet the car, Sadiah moved to a chair opposite the room's open door. Quietly, Cord and Dimo took position one on either side of the doorway. In a few moments there were fresh footsteps in the hall, and they heard Karog's clipped, impersonal voice.

"Admittedly, it was not convenient, but as Miss Shellon was so insistent . . ." the soldier, immaculate as ever, let the sentence die as he entered the room and saw Sadiah. "Miss Beh, this is a surprise."

"And life's full of them." From behind him, Cord's warning came flat and cautionary. The soldier's hand started towards the holster at his side. "No, major — don't be a fool."

Suramo's second-in-command showed himself sensible. His gun-arm moved well clear of his side before he turned. He eyed the two automatics which covered him then swore just once, softly and with a measure of disgust, as Brink and Kate Shellon came in.

"I should have realised. A European is always just that — even you, *dokter*."

Brink winced. Cord stepped forward, removed the revolver from Karog's holster, and thumbed towards a vacant chair. "Sit down."

Scowling, he obeyed. "Now what?"

"Just stay quite still and listen." Cord

nodded to Kate. "Whenever you're ready."

Instead, she glanced at Sadiah. The girl bit her lip but crossed to the table where the tape recorder lay waiting, automatically checked the controls, then pressed the start key. The reels began to turn, the rich, deep voice of Pak Gadjal boomed across the room. At first, Karog's broad, high-boned face remained unchanged. Then, as the words began to register, the cynical indifference faded. After a couple of sentences, his hard, intelligent eyes had narrowed. He leaned forward a little, frowning as he concentrated.

The tape hissed into silence and, as Sadiah stopped the machine, Karog straightened.

"It is some kind of fake."

"Full marks," agreed Dimo cheerfully.

Cord nodded. "Sadiah edited up one of the Gadjal interview tapes. Tell the major why, Sadiah."

"Because it was wanted by Colonel Suramo and the one who calls himself

Allat," she said, her voice low and colourless. "That's why I came to Barumma. The man who calls himself Allat is also the *orang-laut* Captain Muka."

Karog's mouth sagged, then he gave a harsh, indignant growl. "*Masja Allah* . . . you expect me to believe that kind of nonsense?"

"Truth usually tastes raw," rapped Cord. "Major, the original of that tape will start playing over Barumma radio soon after midnight. By then, you're going to be sitting in the middle of a full-scale revolution." He met and held the soldier's caustic, cynical gaze. "At ten tonight they expect a dump of explosives to go up under the Dragon Dancers. In the middle of the panic, an attack will be launched against Pappang's men on Kuwa — with Allat already there to help open the way."

Peter Dimo stepped between them. "Listen, major. You know Suramo — he'll jump in anyone's pocket if the money is right. Well, the price will be a cut from twenty million dollars worth of diamonds. Do you think he'll worry about how he gets it?" His broad, flat nostrils flared indignantly. "Major, I rate you as a realist, and an honest one. Do you want another taste of Stormking nights and village executions, another start to a bloodbath?"

The sheer vehemence in the words had silenced the soldier. Frowning, showing the beginnings of indecision, he looked around him. "All I have heard are words on a tape. Can you show me real proof of any of this?"

"Yes," said Doctor Brink quietly. "I have proof, the kind any man can believe."

He went over to the serving table, lifted a covering napkin, and came back using both hands to nurse the finned tube of the mortar bomb. "I helped dig this up on the Isle of Dragons, major. I saw many more — and I saw three newly dead men. Two of them would have killed us."

Carefully, the soldier examined the

bomb. Beads of sweat had started on his forehead when he handed it back. He pulled out a handkerchief and mopped the moisture.

"Japanese. That part I can understand." He watched anxiously until the bomb had been returned to the table. "You say — you claim there will be this attack on Kuwa. By a handful of *orang-laut* pirates against a full company of infantry?"

"By a force of Huks and PKI," said Cord shortly. "A strong force — some of them are in Barumma now. When it happens, the district troops won't act without Suramo's orders — and as security officer you'll know he's made sure they're mostly out of the area."

"You are well informed." Karog nodded with a grim condescension. He turned towards Kate. "And I suppose you also have a contribution, Miss Shellon?"

"I saw what happened on the island," said the redhead, the lack of emotion in her manner a telling force on its own.

"Two nights back I saw soldiers helping load two *kumpits* at a creek up-river. I didn't imagine these things, major. If you want proof — well, who took Pak Gadjal back to his village?"

"The colonel . . ."

"But did Pak Gadjal arrive there?" she asked.

"What do you mean, Kate?" Cord raised an eyebrow, as puzzled as the rest.

"Would they let him go back, when he could be free to brand that tape as a fake?"

"It makes sense," grated Dimo, snapping finger and thumb together. "It also takes a woman to teach three professionals their business."

"Professionals?" Karog's sigh was genuine. "You are from the Federation, then?"

"From the next-door neighbour," confirmed Dimo with a chuckle. "Talos is different. His pay-cheque comes from the United Nations."

The soldier blinked. "Then why

303

come here, Mr Cord? Even if all the rest is true, I have read your charter. The U.N. has no power, no right to interfere in internal affairs of any nation."

"Depends what you mean by internal." Cord grinned a little. He'd won as far as Karog was concerned, even if the soldier still had to admit it. "If you want chapter and verse, there's Article Thirty-four . . . 'may investigate any dispute or any situation which might lead to international friction or give rise to a dispute, in order to determine whether the continuation of the dispute or situation is likely to endanger the maintenance of international peace and security.' There's plenty more of the same. We discovered a long time ago that it pays to have some elastic in the rules."

"I see." Wearily, Karog fitted a cigarette into his tortoise-shell holder. Cord deliberately laid down the Neuhausen, took out his lighter, and flicked it to life.

"You've known something was shaping, haven't you, major?"

"*Ja.*" The admission came reluctantly and with it the last of Karog's opposition crumbled. He touched his cigarette to the flame and took a long, unhappy draw. "There have been signs. Suramo laughed at me when I reported them. You have — well, more to your story?"

"A lot more."

"Then we accept each other." The soldier rose to his feet. "But there is something I must do — my driver has his orders if I do not rejoin him inside ten minutes." He glanced almost sheepishly towards Kate. "I take precautions, no matter how attractive a messenger comes. And perhaps I can clear up one matter. It should take him about an hour to check at Pak Gadjal's village."

"You trust your driver?" queried Brink.

Karog nodded. "He is my sister's husband — it helps."

305

They let him go. In a minute or so the station wagon drove off and Karog returned with a purposeful air.

"And now, Mr Cord . . ."

"You won't like some of it," warned Dimo.

Karog gave a minimal shrug. "I have very little surprise left in me. At noon, for some mysterious reason, the army transmitter in Barumma broke down. This week several of my best men have been transferred to other units by Suramo. That is part of why I decided to believe you, so go on."

They told him. By the time they'd finished his controlled veneer was close to cracking.

"Then the Tan Sallong Society has been the front for their organisation . . ."

"Here and in other places," nodded Cord. "They've a few innocent members, but the majority are like Suramo and your plain-clothes sergeant."

The soldier scowled. "I can warn Colonel Pappang. There is a direct line to Kuwa from my office, and

Pappang has his own transmitter. He can contact Djakarta."

"Provided his transmitter still works," murmured Brink. "The same thing probably applies to the civil cable line."

Hopefully, Sadiah leaned forward. "You could send messengers to the nearest of the army units outside Barumma, calling them back . . ."

"True. But would they act without Suramo's direct orders?" Karog shook his head. "A few perhaps, but not many. It is always safer to obey your commander than to listen to a wild tale from his second-in-command." He brightened slightly. "At least there will be no signal from the Isle of Dragons."

"But they'll still go ahead with the attack," emphasised Cord. "Allat will have to alter his plans, alter them drastically, but he can still pull it off. Knowing Dimo and I are loose is enough for him to be ready for surprises." He stopped, suddenly frowning, then grabbed at the idea beginning to shape in his mind. "Major, I think I've got a starting point. Maybe there should be some kind of an explosion out on the Isle of Dragons. And I'd better give you back your gun. Once Dimo and I get changed back into our usual clothes you're going to arrest us."

"Eh?" Karog wasn't the only one who appeared dazed.

Cord thumped his fist on the table. "We came to ask Doctor Brink's help. But he tipped you off instead — so you take us into Barumma, tuck us into a cell, and we're nice and handy for a little later."

He talked on. Gradually Karog's expression moved through doubt to reluctant acceptance.

"We have a saying, Mr Cord," he mused grimly. "*Orang harus mati* . . . man must die. That is what will happen if this fails. But if we win . . . " he slapped his thigh at the notion.

***

Karog's corporal brother-in-law returned on schedule. His report was brief and positive — Pak Gadjal hadn't been seen in his home village since the morning he'd left for Barumma.

For the rest, they were ready. Handcuffed together, Cord and Dimo climbed into the back seat. They said a quick good-bye to Brink and the girls then, as the station wagon started on the road to Barumma, Karog gave his brother-in-law a list of instructions which made the man's eyes bulge with surprise.

Karog's uniform and the handcuffs were their passport through the roadblock on the fringe of town. Then the station wagon crawled through the crowded streets and at last pulled up outside the two-storey civil security headquarters.

"My apologies in advance," murmured Karog briefly. He jumped out of the car, waved the waiting sentry to join him, and made a realistic job of dragging

309

Cord and Dimo out into the sunlight.

From there, they were pushed and shoved into the building. Within moments, the main corridor seemed filled with uniformed men, all talking at once.

"Silence!" Karog's voice was an angry bellow. "Take these two and lock them up. No, you fool . . . .." he glared as a private made to search his prisoners " . . . I have taken care of that. One of you get a message to Colonel Suramo. Tell him we have the European and his accomplice. The rest of you, back to work."

He stalked off towards his office, leaving Cord and Dimo to be prodded deeper along the corridor, down a short flight of steps to a lower level, then finally shoved into a cell with a solid metal door and a single, narrow window-slit. Their handcuffs were removed, the escort retreated, and the door slammed shut.

The cell had a small wooden bench under the window and a bucket in one corner. Dimo stood on the bench, peered out through the window-slit, and grimaced.

"All I can see is someone's washing." He stepped down again, shaking his head. "I have done some crazy things, but this beats all records."

"It could be worse." Cord pointed to one wall. Some previous occupant had scratched the outline of a gallows on the grey cement, but the little man dangling from the noose hadn't been completed.

Half an hour passed before they heard footsteps outside. The footsteps stopped, a spyhole in the cell door flipped open, and they had a brief glimpse of an eye peering in. The man moved away and another eye took his place. Seconds later the spyhole clicked shut once more and the footsteps moved away.

After that, as the minutes crawled past, Cord gradually sensed a little of Dimo's uneasiness creeping into his own mind. But at last, as the hands of his watch crept up towards six, the corridor outside erupted into a sudden, noisy bedlam. Doors opened and slammed then, above the sounds of loud protests and scuffling, they heard a single pistol-shot. The bedlam died, a key rattled, and their cell door swung open.

"We are ready now, I think." Major Karog beamed in, revolver in one hand, his uniform slightly dishevelled. "And — ah — we could use this accommodation."

They needed no second invitation. As they came out, two of Karog's men used the butts of their carbines to hustle a trio of battered, bleeding captives into the cell. Behind them, another figure lay silent on the concrete floor. More of Karog's men waited nearby.

"Looks like you had a little trouble," said Dimo politely.

"A little." Karog thumbed to the figure on the floor. "That one had a knife, and decided to use it. The others who might have similar thoughts are either taken care of or being collected now — and the rest are men I can be certain about. Some of them are already busy."

"Who looked in earlier?" queried Cord.

"Suramo and Allat. But let's leave this place."

They followed him up to his room, past a succession of armed men. Once there, Karog gestured towards the desk. Their guns lay waiting.

"Let me start with Suramo." The soldier prowled the room in restless fashion. "He congratulated me on your capture — so did Allat. Then, as we agreed, I told him you had tried to convince me of some wild tale." He chuckled briefly. "When I produced the tape they grabbed it from me."

"Any orders about us?" queried Cord.

"Interesting ones. Suramo claims that cabled instructions from Djakarta mean he will be unable to go to the Isle of

313

Dragons as he'd planned. Instead, we meet here at nine tonight, when you will be interrogated." Karog sniffed and gestured angrily. "Mr Cord, the cable line went out of action this morning. Suramo has received no instructions from outside — no one can contact Barumma."

"Except maybe through Pappang," murmured Dimo.

"No." Karog's eyes hardened. "Let me explain the rest first. There were a few men of whom I could be sure. Two went with my brother-in-law to the Isle of Dragons to prepare our substitute explosion. That left me three — for their first task I ordered them to burgle the Tan Sallong Society office."

"In daylight?" Dimo's eyes opened wide behind the spectacles.

"On a public holiday," corrected Karog. "It was closed of course — and they brought back the membership list. It made unhappy reading. I have fifty men under my direct command, and twelve were listed. They are the ones now being locked away in our cells. But I could not do that until Suramo had gone, and I could not contact Colonel Pappang until then. My switchboard operator was on that list."

Cord tried to fight back his impatience. "But when you spoke to Pappang?"

"He believed me. He had reason — his own transmitter was sabotaged this afternoon." Karog gave a long sigh and leaned against his desk. "So we are cut off, absolutely. But at least Colonel Pappang's force will be ready — and Allat will be arrested the moment he arrives on Kuwa. Pappang understands the rest, and wishes us luck."

"Which we'll need." Cord went through the motions of lighting a cheroot, his mind busy. "What about the local army units?"

"The Tan Sallong Society list contains some surprising names," said Karog bitterly. "But I have sent word to three units, ordering them to return to positions near town. The commander of one unit is a friend — I have told him more than the others." He shrugged. "We will see. There is another matter. When Doctor Brink and the ladies arrive I have to assign Sergeant Laye as their escort for the evening. Laye is the man who shadowed you — he is downstairs with the rest. I will arrange a substitute."

Cord nodded. In less than two hours it would be dusk and the boats would begin leaving for the Isle of Dragons. In less than four hours . . .

He crossed to the window, looked out over the town, and thought of the broadcasting station above their heads.

"Seen anything of Janos Manton?"

"If you bored a hole through this ceiling you would look into his office," grimaced Karog. "He visited me earlier when he heard you were captured. But forget him for now. His station has a separate entrance and this area is now closed to outsiders. If there are questions, it is because of the dangerous prisoners we hold."

"Namely us," murmured Dimo with a mild satisfaction. "Talos, why can't we just grab Manton's transmitter and try shouting for help over the public broadcasting wavelength?"

"Because we'd tip our hand," said Cord brusquely. "Five minutes after we started we'd have a worse mess than ever breaking over us."

Dimo shrugged. "Major, I feel like some exercise — and the streets are busy enough for it to be safe. If you'll give me someone to run courier I'll keep an eye around the harbour area. I know the faces we should be seeing."

It made sense. He left with a bulky plain-clothes corporal in tow, and for Cord the worst of the waiting began.

At seven-thirty, while the sun gradually edged down towards the horizon, the first word came back from the army units. A mechanised half-company was already on the move. Messages from the other two units contacted followed within minutes. One would come in as ordered, but the tone was reluctant.

317

The second, with Karog's friend in command, would be ready to strike from the edge of town any time after nine.

As dusk fell, an orderly brought in coffee and small, sweet cakes. With them came a scribbled note from Peter Dimo. He reckoned the Tengah yard now held roughly a hundred men and had marked several small groups around the harbour area.

"For the causeway," said Karog grimly. "But I still say the main attack will come from the sea."

Standing at the window, Cord nodded. The distant braying of horns and trumpets was adding a new dimension to the noise coming from the town. "It's going to be quite a night," he said softly. "Let's hope you're not backing the losing side."

"It would be a little late for such thoughts," murmured Karog. "Except, perhaps, for you — you have no particular stake in all this." He stopped, then sucked his teeth apologetically.

"No, perhaps that is wrong. But someday I will ask you why, if there is a chance."

Minutes before eight, Doctor Brink arrived with Kate and Sadiah. Both girls were laden down with recording gear. They listened quietly to Cord's instructions, nodded their understanding, and only Brink made a protest.

"I would be of more use here . . ."

"Not if we want everything to look natural," emphasised Cord. "Doctor, given some luck we may manage to do more than just stifle this thing. We'll have the chance to smash it, prevent the same people trying it somewhere else in a few months' time." He glanced at the girls. "Remember the rest. Once you get out to the island you'll join up with the rest of Karog's men. Whatever happens, get clear and stay hidden when the deadline comes round. The explosion will be on an empty beach, and if Allat has any men landed among the Dragon Dancers they'll come looking to find out what's gone wrong. Don't take chances."

As Karog escorted Brink and Sadiah out of the office to their waiting car Kate Shellon hung back.

"What kind of chances will you be taking, Talos?" she asked quietly.

"Not one more than I can help." Cord put his hands on her shoulders. "Kate, I learned a long time ago that there's no particular dividend in sticking your neck out without reason." He kissed her, hard and quickly, then grinned.

With a forced, hopeful smile she headed after the others.

★ ★ ★

The first of the Isle of Dragons flotilla began to leave as darkness arrived. From Karog's window, the spectacle amounted to a bright, flickering movement of torches as the crowds at the harbour began to embark, then more patterns of light as one by one the boats headed out to sea. Dimo's next note reported that Kate and the others were on their way. Twenty minutes later, he returned in person and entered the room as Major Karog laid down the telephone receiver on his desk.

"That's it," declared Dimo. "Allat's crossed the causeway to Kuwa with the rest of the diamond buyers. Fourteen of them in three cars."

"Thirteen now," corrected Karog briskly. "That was Colonel Pappang. Allat is under arrest — and protesting loudly."

Thirteen was unlucky for some. Cord glanced once more at his watch, wondering just which way that bad luck was heading.

"So what's next on the agenda?" asked Dimo cheerfully.

"You deal with the radio station five minutes after Suramo gets here," Cord told him. "There's a squad waiting — and remember Manton's office is up above this one. A little demonstration would oblige."

The young Malaysian grinned his understanding.

Whatever else might be said about him, Colonel Suramo believed in punctuality. Exactly on nine o'clock a small convoy of vehicles swept towards the security block. A jeep with a mounted machine-gun led the way, followed by Suramo's car. Bringing up the rear, a lumbering half-track halted behind the others and disgorged a section of heavily-armed infantry who lined up under an n.c.o.

Two of the infantrymen at his heels, Suramo entered the building. A few seconds later, when he flung open Major Karog's door without knocking, it was to find Karog at his desk, a masterly look of surprise on his face.

"Colonel . . . " Karog pushed aside the paperwork in front of him with one hand and started to rise to his feet. "I hadn't realised the time . . . "

Suramo grunted and stumped in, his two bodyguards close behind. "You have Cord and Dimo ready?"

"Yes, Colonel." For the first time, Karog brought his left hand into view. A percussion grenade poised delicately in his fingertips, he glared past Suramo at the infantrymen. "*Djangan!* If this should drop . . . "

The men froze. Suramo swallowed hard and lumbered another step forward. "Karog, are you mad?"

"If he is, he's got company," rapped Cord from behind.

The district governor swivelled round. In the doorway, Cord was flanked on either side by one of Karog's men — each with a Sten gun held at chest height, finger on trigger.

"You seemed shocked, Colonel," murmured Karog. "I suggest you sit down."

The two infantrymen, stripped of their weapons, were shoved out into the corridor. Cord closed the door and leaned back against it.

"The man invited you to sit, Colonel."

"*Ja.*" The broad, fleshy face quivered

a little as, breathing heavily, Suramo took the waiting chair. "But you are fools. I have support in this building, a squad outside . . . "

"The first has been dealt with, the second . . . " Karog crossed to the window and looked out. "They have been told you want them inside. They are coming. All of them. Yes, the last one enters now." Something in the man's manner made Cord feel suddenly cold.

Suramo started to speak. But the words vanished, wiped out by an instant, clattering heat of machine-gun fire, a beat which echoed through the building. They heard screams, the gun pulsed on — then it stopped and left a terrible silence.

"Hell, if you've . . . " Cord let the words die, stared at the soldier, then swung to open the door.

"Mr Cord!" Karog's voice cracked like a whip. "I did not like it either. But we can cope with no more prisoners."

White-faced, Cord slowly took his

hand from the door. "It was plain butchery . . . "

"I agree." Karog said it simply, but his fingers shook as he carefully reinserted the pin in the grenade and laid it in front of him. "But if it was heard outside then this man's friends would presume it was us who died. Mr Cord, I have no stronger stomach than the next man — which is why this pig in front of me makes me feel sick by his presence." Eyes blazing, he glared at Suramo.

"You — you are my second-in-command." The district governor's voice quivered, each word an effort. "Whatever they have told you . . . "

"Told?" Karog snorted. "Colonel, understand this. I know, Pappang on Kuwa knows and your friend Allat has been seized. If the rest is to be *tewas*, if we are to die, then you will be with us."

Suramo's face had greyed. Desperately, he moistened his thick lips. "You could still join us, both of you. Karog, they have force enough to crush any opposition here. But if — if you join us, I can promise . . . " he broke off as, above their heads, a series of muted thumps spelled out an erratic V in Morse.

Composed again, Karog gave a wolfish grin. "Your answer, Colonel. We have the radio station, which means no Pak Gadjal broadcast." He stood over the fat, frightened figure, his words raking like steel claws. "And tonight, when your signal comes from the Isle of Dragons, it will come from my men."

"Which leaves us with just one immediate puzzle, Colonel," mused Cord. "That's what to do with you."

"A pity he will never get to use these bank accounts," nodded Karog, almost over-playing it. "All those years of graft and corruption — to end with a bullet through that fat belly."

Suramo cringed, saliva starting to trickle from one corner of his mouth. "At least a trial . . ."

Cord decided the time was ripe, glanced at Karog, and received the faintest of nods. "Still, maybe we could make some kind of deal with him. For instance, Colonel, if you knew Allat's attack plan."

"*Ja*, I do." The man nodded quickly and eagerly.

"Then you tell us. Karog's got the best part of two companies of infantry moving in, so you sign orders authorising them to act under his command, and other orders to any other units we can contact. Where's Pak Gadjal?"

"Safe — under guard in a house in town."

"That helps." Cord drew out the Neuhausen and swung it lightly by the trigger guard. "We'll fetch him here, and as soon as the shooting starts you'll go on the air with him and make a little speech. You'll tell the people not to panic, that they've got to rise up and help the army against the PKI bandits. And you'll make it good, because there'll be a gun right behind you."

Alarm flared in Suramo's eyes. "But if I do that, then afterwards what — what happens to me?"

"You'll be top of the Huk and PKI hate list." snapped Cord. "But your government might even give you a medal to mark your resignation and retiral."

Behind them, the door was flung open. Peter Dimo stood there, looking at them with blank horror in his eyes. "Talos, outside in the corridor . . ."

"Major Karog decided it was necessary," said Cord heavily.

"They're tidying it up, but . . ." Dimo fought the picture from his mind. "We — we got the radio station, nothing damaged except Manton. I had to knock him around a little." He pointed towards Suramo. "What about him?"

"Let's find out," said Cord softly. "Well, Colonel?"

Slowly, reluctantly, Suramo nodded.

★ ★ ★

Five minutes later, as Suramo finished answering their questions on Allat's attack positions, a three-man infantry patrol reached the security block. The first of the district units was in position outside town.

By nine thirty, Suramo's signed authorisations were on their way and with them Karog's hastily drafted battle orders. The Huk and PKI bands were in three concentrations, the smallest gathered near the causeway for a direct attack which would be a covering feint for the real thrusts, coastal landings by *orang-laut* boats from north and south, a pincer move to hit the causeway defenders from the rear. The causeway attack would begin five minutes after the Isle of Dragons explosion, the coastal landing ten minutes later.

Karog's plan was crude but practical. One concentration of his enemy was waiting at the hidden creek on the River Ular, the second force would embark from a small bay south of Barumma. He would concentrate on complete destruction of the Ular group before they sailed and, once the causeway attack had begun, in hitting that force from the rear. Colonel Pappang would have to meet the attack from the south on his own, at least till the mainland situation was resolved.

The telephone cable to Kuwa still operated. Cord listened to Karog's crisp appraisal to the Javanese colonel at the other end then, as the telephone went down, Karog gave a faint sigh.

"Something wrong?"

The soldier shook his head. "No. For the first time I think we have more than a chance — much more." He looked around. "Where's Dimo?"

"Gone with a couple of your men to get Pak Gadjal." Cord thumbed towards Suramo, sitting gloomily in one corner. "We thought it was time our district governor started rehearsals."

"Good." Karog grinned and lit a cigarette, then raised an eyebrow as the telephone shrilled. He picked it up. "*Ja?*"

Watching, Cord saw the soldier's face give a sudden twitch of surprise. Karog shot a swift question, listened intently, then suddenly swore and thumbed the receiver rest in rapid urgency. At last, slowly, he laid the receiver down again.

"Allat is free — that was Colonel Pappang again. It has just happened."

"What?" Cord took a moment to grasp the reality.

"We forgot the man who sabotaged the Kuwa transmitter," said Karog softly. "Allat's guard was shot. He is loose somewhere on the island — and now the line is dead." He scowled across at Suramo. "Cut?"

Suramo nodded unhappily. "It was ordered for twelve minutes before the explosion was due."

Cord drew a deep breath. "Major, I want to borrow that jeep outside. I'm going to try the causeway."

"Now?" Karog's broad, flat face

conveyed the distinct impression that he regarded the idea as madness. "Why?"

"Because Allat's not fighting now. He's running, and he'll have an escape route ready — he's not the kind to take chances. Look, there's no attack coming from the Isle of Dragons. Why? Because that's his bolthole. If he gets there, he gets free and there can be another time. Or if he meets up with Kate or Sadiah . . . "

"Pappang . . . "

"Pappang can't afford the men." Cord forestalled further argument. "I'll take Suramo as my passport — Allat's men will let him through. Now, do I get the jeep?"

Biting lightly on his lip, Karog nodded.

"*Tidak* . . . no," protested Suramo. "We will both die . . . "

"Not if you do what you're told," grated Cord. "But don't try to be clever. You'll have a gun six inches from your spine."

332

Eight minutes were left when Cord gunned the jeep away from the security building and, headlights glaring, sent it roaring through the deserted streets. He wore an army cap and jacket and Suramo sat beside him, bolt upright in the passenger seat. Crouched low at the rear, a corporal had the barrel of a Sten jammed between the front seats, the muzzle jammed against the colonel's back.

They travelled fast, without hindrance. For reasons best known to itself Barumma, the Dragon Dancers gone, had suddenly shut its doors and barred its windows — a town which knew a fury was about to break. But whoever saw them, whoever might have trained a sight on the speeding vehicle, the sheer audacity of its blatant progress removed suspicion.

Five minutes left, they raced past the harbour, the pier reaching out into the night like a long black finger, the causeway's dark shadow ahead. The jeep's lights shone on a figure with a carbine, one hand waving them to halt, the message backed by a medium machine-gun and crew a few feet to one side.

Cord slowed the jeep to a crawl, nudged Suramo hard, and watched the figures ahead. The uniforms were the shapeless, dark-green overalls of the Huks and Muka's men, the faces a shadowed blur. Suramo stood up, clutching the jeep's windscreen, his legs trembling.

"*Menepilah*!" Suramo's voice held a hoarse, desperate authority. "You know me — I have to get to Captain Muka. An emergency. *Menepilah* . . . move clear!"

The man with the carbine hesitated, peered closer, then sprang back. Cord let in the clutch with a thump, rammed down on the accelerator, and the jeep lunged forward. Dark figures were gathered at the edge of the road, he heard confused shouts — and the causeway was there. He swung the wheel, the jeep's tyres screamed, then they were racing across with water on either side while he prayed that Pappang's men wouldn't decide to squash this early, glaring-eyed invader.

One third of the way across, a rifle blasted from the Barumma side followed by another — and next moment a ragged fury of fire was whining around them. Allat's men had changed their decision. In the rear seat, the corporal tossed the Sten aside, grabbed the jeep's mounted machinegun, and began pouring a wild, hosing reply of tracer bullets. The windscreen glass shattered, a hot knife seemed to slice along the top of Cord's shoulder, and Suramo pitched forward.

The corporal had stopped firing and was moaning. But their headlamps shone on an opened barricade and as the jeep skidded through a new racket of small-arms fire broke out. The Kuwa defenders were opening up on their still unseen enemy. As Cord stopped, men in uniform swarmed around and a loud, insistent voice shouted for the vehicle's lights to be put out.

He answered someone's questions while Suramo and the corporal were lifted down. The firing began to fade — and a slim, slight figure pushed its way towards him. Colonel Pappang appeared younger than ever beneath a steel helmet, and his face was a mixture of anger and puzzlement.

"You have some important reason for this, Cord? Our plan . . . "

"Was before you lost Allat," snapped Cord in turn. He swung his legs out of the jeep and faced the island's commandant, feeling the hot, sticky trickle of blood from his shoulder soaking down his back. "Allat matters — and I know where he has to be heading." He glanced at his watch. There was less than a minute to go.

"Allat — that is different." Pappang's scowl became several degrees friendlier. "The man who helped him was wounded and captured, but . . . " the rest was obliterated as a deep, reverberating blast split the night air. Every face turned towards the Isle of Dragons, where a bright orange glow rose in the sky. As it died, a fresh outbreak of firing broke out from the causeway. Whatever confusion existed on the mainland, the signal had settled matters.

"We are ready for them." Pappang's teeth flashed in a hard, mirthless grin. "I can guess what Allat's role would have been — the causeway sentries. When we searched him, he had a Woodsman pistol and silencer."

Behind them, the Kuwa force had begun returning fire. A Verey light soared into the sky, the sputtering glare showing a bunched group of men scurrying along the causeway. They melted as the infantry carbines began snapping and were joined by the throb of a heavy machine-gun.

"I reckon Allat's heading for the Isle of Dragons," yelled Cord above the din. "Probably for an emergency pick-up. I told Karog you wouldn't have the men . . . "

"For a search?" Pappang shook his head. "I need all I have, here and for the south defence. But — yes, I can spare perhaps two." He turned, shouted, and two figures hurried over. "Lieutenant Maung and his sergeant will go with you." He pointed to Cord's shoulder. "I would let one of them drive — and take care. Allat is armed again."

"Thanks."

Pappang shook his head. "Get him for me, Mr Cord. That is all I ask." He spoke quickly to Maung and the sergeant, then strode away.

The sergeant took the wheel, Cord beside him, the young lieutenant perched behind them. The jeep growled off, gathering speed along the track, sweeping past the low barrack blocks, its lights quickly picking out the first of the diamond pits and their fringing spoil-heaps. Behind them, the noise of battle was still loud — and looking north, towards the mainland, Cord could see faint, distant flashes which showed that the Ular invaders were already being tackled by Major Karog's force.

Maung leaned forward. "He would not stay with the track. The direct way is quicker — but we can follow. *Sekarang* . . . now!"

Obediently, their driver fed the wheel through his fingers and the jeep swung off, bouncing over the rough ground, threading between the diamond pits, wheels jumping, tyres clipping unseen obstacles and spattering the soft soil. The headlamps glared on more and more heaps of spoil.

"This section is worked out," said Maung briefly. "You understand we need the headlights?"

"Keep them," nodded Cord. "If I'm right, he'll keep going whether he sees or hears us." Then, as the jeep shuddered on, now close to the shore, he suddenly frowned, straining his hearing, trying to locate another throb he'd become conscious of above the vehicle's growl.

"Pull up." He signalled the sergeant to halt, leaned over, and switched off engine and lights.

Maung half-rose. "What . . . "

He silenced the lieutenant with a shake of his head. He could hear it plainly now, the steady thump of a powerful marine diesel, and not far distant. Beside him, the sergeant grunted and pointed. The dark shape of a *kumpit* was out there, heading in at an angle towards the shore.

"Your friend's lifeboat," muttered Maung with a grim satisfaction. "But at that heading, it will still be on Kuwa they will meet, not the Isle of Dragons."

"*Tuan?*" The sergeant glanced eagerly at Cord.

He nodded, the engine fired and, headlamps blazing again, they were off, racing the *kumpit*, slowed by the old diamond pits all around. Cord heard the loud click as Maung checked the jeep's machine-gun, and guessed that pretty much the same thing must be happening aboard the boat.

They saw Allat less than a minute later, suddenly silhouetted by the headlamps, running hard, heading for the beach. He skidded to a halt, his arm rose, and a shot whined over their heads. Two hundred yards off shore, the *kumpit*'s crew saw their captain's plight. The boat's spotlight flared to life, sweeping in to home on the jeep. A savage burst of automatic fire rasped from near the bow, bullets kicking the ground a few yards short and to the rear.

"*Disitu* . . . over there!" Maung swore, pointed, then scrambled for the jeep's gun as his sergeant spun the wheel and shot the little vehicle behind the cover of the nearest spoil-heap. Another long burst of automatic fire whined around.

"Lieutenant . . . " Cord grabbed the man by the arm " . . . hold them off, and I'll get Allat."

Maung nodded, already reaching for the cocking handle as Cord jumped out and began running. A little way ahead, Allat's gun barked twice, the reports almost lost as the jeep's heavy-calibre weapon opened up. Maung's first long, searching burst of tracer brought immediate results. The *kumpit*'s spotlight vanished with a smash of glass.

But Cord ignored the duel. Neuhausen in hand, he sprinted on, saw a vague movement ahead, took a quick snap-shot, and knew he'd missed. Next moment the Indonesian had vanished, diving behind another spoil-heap. Cord threw himself into a frantic zig-zag, heard a bullet scream close to his head, then lunged for cover as another shot followed.

He landed heavily on a mass of soft spoil and hugged it lovingly, breathing hard, the Neuhausen half-buried beside him. The jeep's gun was hammering away, four belt-fed rounds per second, every fourth a tracer, pounding away in a monotonous beat of cyclic rhythm. And, though the *kumpit* still answered, the return fire was weakening, the boat was veering away from that vicious storm of lead raking along its length.

Allat saw — and understood. He broke cover, running for the beach, arms waving. Cord sprang up, triggered the Neuhausen, and cursed as it jammed, fouled by the adhering earth. But the *kumpit* was plainly turning, had stopped firing . . .

"Captain Muka!" Cord howled the words above the frenetic din. Allat stopped, looked round despairingly, then, as Cord raced towards him, his gun-arm came up again.

The first shot plucked at Cord's clothing, then he catapulted forward the remaining distance to hit the man in a flying tackle below the waist. The gun exploded wildly as they went down together, rolling on the ground, a strange, non-stop sobbing coming from Allat's lips as they struggled.

A knee crashed into Cord's stomach, low and hard enough to force the breath from his body. The revolver in

Allat's right hand was twisting round to bear while the man's left scratched for his eyes. Cord chopped at Allat's throat, his other hand closing like an iron band on the gun wrist, twisting, forcing the muzzle back. They rolled again . . .

And, suddenly, they were falling, falling amid a splintering of wood while Allat screamed. Cord was on top as they hit the bottom of the old diamond pit amidst a downpour of sand and gravel and rotted timber slatting. More was coming loose, the whole side of the fifteen-foot deep pit was beginning to crumble. Allat screamed again, then the only fight was to get clear from the rushing, clogging mass as it collapsed towards them. A timber hit him hard on the chest. Something was gripping his foot. He kicked desperately, struggled to heave himself clear — and saw the black mass of soil crashing towards him. His eyes and mouth were blocked, the world was a roaring, stifling darkness . . .

★ ★ ★

Vaguely, he'd been aware of brief moments when things were happening and he'd felt pain. But, when the darkness at last fully receded, it gave way to the bright glare of an overhead light and the soft murmur of voices. He was in a room, his body ached all over, his left leg felt numb and strangely heavy.

Slowly, almost reluctantly, Cord forced his eyes open and focused on the figures around him. He was in a bed. The room was small, the walls painted cream, and Major Karog was looking down at him. He tried to rise, and winced as a little man with a large hammer started work inside his head.

"Welcome back," said Peter Dimo's voice with a cheerful thankfulness. "You're the ugliest looking piece of buried treasure I've seen salvaged, but you'll do."

Cord tried again, and managed to prop up on his elbows. Dimo was sitting on the end of the bed. A white-coated army orderly was moving around in the background, and Major Karog's white-toothed grin was wide and friendly.

"It's over?"

"Over many hours," nodded Karog with a happy satisfaction. "For you, Talos, it is now tomorrow afternoon. And we smashed them. Those that weren't killed at the Ular or the causeways surrendered. The southern group didn't even attempt to land on Kuwa, and there are patrol boats out from Celebes and the south picking up the ones who escaped. They have already captured Muka's *kumpit* — and what men are left on it."

Cord gave a sigh. "What about Suramo?"

"He will live — and for political reasons may get that medal you suggested." Karog grimaced. "Still, the rest is finished. Pak Gadjal had broadcast every hour, the few small uprisings inland have melted."

346

"Good." Cord eased himself into a slightly more comfortable position. "And Allat, Muka, whatever we should call him?"

Peter Dimo cleared his throat and carefully adjusted his spectacles. "That was different, Talos. Maung and his sergeant somehow managed to dig down to you, but they had problems getting you out. That's why you've got a broken leg. Allat had to wait till later, a lot later. He was dead."

"But we know from Suramo who he was," growled Karog. "His real name was Tjimpa, an old PKI leader from Sumatra. The real Allat is dead, murdered. For the diamond merchant Chou Sie it was the same fate once they brought him ashore from the *Tari* — though Suramo claims he thought they would only hold the old man prisoner. We will recover the body."

The soldier stopped, then shrugged and grimaced awkwardly. "There now exists a slight difficulty. You will understand that, officially, neither you nor Dimo can exist in any reports. Colonel Pappang and I will handle matters with discretion, but an investigating commission is on its way . . ."

"In other words, they want us to get to hell out of it," said Dimo wryly. "You're fit to travel, and the *Tari*'s waiting. So's somebody else. But . . ." he chuckled " . . . that plaster on your leg's going to slow down the action."

"A lady should never be kept waiting," murmured Karog. Solemnly, he drew out a small, crumpled envelope and laid it on the bedsheet. "Pappang asked that I give you this. He said you once mentioned a possible use for the contents."

Cord opened the envelope and looked inside. Uncut diamonds in their raw state have little glitter or glamour, and the pair in the envelope were moderately sized. But even to his inexpert eye they were well matched for size and quality.

"Tell the colonel I appreciate his

thoughtfulness," he said solemnly.

As the two men went out, followed by the orderly, he rubbed a hand over his unshaven chin. All he had to do now was find a craftsman who could create one pair of diamond ear-rings with suitable haste.

The door opened again and he grinned as Kate Shellon's red hair glinted in the overhead light. All right, so his leg was broken. But he had a feeling she had the makings of a particularly sympathetic nurse.

He beckoned her nearer.

Now seemed as good a time as any to find out.

THE END

A FOOT IN THE GRAVE
Bruce Marshall

About to be imprisoned and tortured in Buenos Aires, John Smith escapes, only to become involved in an aeroplane hijacking.

DEAD TROUBLE
Martin Carroll

Trespassing brought Jennifer Denning more than she bargained for. She was totally unprepared for the violence which was to lie in her path.

HOURS TO KILL
Ursula Curtiss

Margaret went to New Mexico to look after her sick sister's rented house and felt a sharp edge of fear when the absent landlady arrived.

THE DEATH OF ABBE DIDIER
Richard Grayson

Inspector Gautier of the Sûreté investigates three crimes which are strangely connected.

NIGHTMARE TIME
Hugh Pentecost

Have the missing major and his wife met with foul play somewhere in the Beaumont Hotel, or is their disappearance a carefully planned step in an act of treason?

BLOOD WILL OUT
Margaret Carr

Why was the manor house so oddly familiar to Elinor Howard? Who would have guessed that a Sunday School outing could lead to murder?

THE DRACULA MURDERS
Philip Daniels

The Horror Ball was interrupted by a spectral figure who warned the merrymakers they were tampering with the unknown.

THE LADIES
OF LAMBTON GREEN
Liza Shepherd

Why did murdered Robin Colquhoun's picture pose such a threat to the ladies of Lambton Green?

CARNABY
AND THE GAOLBREAKERS
Peter N. Walker

Detective Sergeant James Aloysius Carnaby-King is sent to prison as bait. When he joins in an escape he is thrown headfirst into a vicious murder hunt.

MUD IN HIS EYE
Gerald Hammond

The harbourmaster's body is found mangled beneath Major Smyle's yacht. What is the sinister significance of the illicit oysters?

THE SCAVENGERS
Bill Knox

Among the masses of struggling fish in the *Tecta*'s nets was a larger, darker, ominously motionless form . . . the body of a skin diver.

DEATH IN ARCADY
Stella Phillips

Detective Inspector Matthew Furnival works unofficially with the local police when a brutal murder takes place in a caravan camp.

STORM CENTRE
Douglas Clark

Detective Chief Superintendent Masters, temporarily lecturing in a police staff college, finds there's more to the job than a few weeks relaxation in a rural setting.

THE MANUSCRIPT MURDERS
Roy Harley Lewis

Antiquarian bookseller Matthew Coll, acquires a rare 16th century manuscript. But when the Dutch professor who had discovered the journal is murdered, Coll begins to doubt its authenticity.

SHARENDEL
Margaret Carr

Ruth didn't want all that money. And she didn't want Aunt Cass to die. But at Sharendel things looked different. She began to wonder if she had a split personality.

MURDER TO BURN
Laurie Mantell

Sergeants Steven Arrow and Lance Brendon, of the New Zealand police force, come upon a woman's body in the water. When the dead woman is identified they begin to realise that they are investigating a complex fraud.

YOU CAN HELP ME
Maisie Birmingham

Whilst running the Citizens' Advice Bureau, Kate Weatherley is attacked with no apparent motive. Then the body of one of her clients is found in her room.

DAGGERS DRAWN
Margaret Carr

Stacey Manston was the kind of girl who could take most things in her stride, but three murders were something different . . .

THE MONTMARTRE MURDERS
Richard Grayson

Inspector Gautier of Sûreté investigates the disappearance of artist Théo, the heir to a fortune.

GRIZZLY TRAIL
Gwen Moffat

Miss Pink, alone in the Rockies, helps in a search for missing hikers, solves two cruel murders and has the most terrifying experience of her life when she meets a grizzly bear!

BLINDMAN'S BLUFF
Margaret Carr

Kate Deverill had considered suicide. It was one way out — and preferable to being murdered.

BEGOTTEN MURDER
Martin Carroll

When Susan Phillips joined her aunt on a voyage of 12,000 miles from her home in Melbourne, she little knew their arrival would germinate the seeds of murder planted long ago.

WHO'S THE TARGET?
Margaret Carr

Three people whom Abby could identify as her parents' murderers wanted her dead, but she decided that maybe Jason could have been the target.

THE LOOSE SCREW
Gerald Hammond

After a motor smash, Beau Pepys and his cousin Jacqueline, her fiancé and dotty mother, suspect that someone had prearranged the death of their friend. But who, and why?

CASE WITH THREE HUSBANDS
Margaret Erskine

Was it a ghost of one of Rose Bonner's late husbands that gave her old Aunt Agatha such a terrible shock and then murdered her in her bed?

THE END OF THE RUNNING
Alan Evans

Lang continued to push the men and children on and on. Behind them were the men who were hunting them down, waiting for the first signs of exhaustion before they pounced.

CARNABY AND THE HIJACKERS
Peter N. Walker

When Commander Pigeon assigns Detective Sergeant Carnaby-King to prevent a raid on a bullion-carrying passenger train, he knows that there are traitors in high positions.

TREAD WARILY AT MIDNIGHT
Margaret Carr

If Joanna Morse hadn't been so hasty she wouldn't have been involved in the accident.

TOO BEAUTIFUL TO DIE
Martin Carroll

There was a grave in the churchyard to prove Elizabeth Weston was dead. Alive, she presented a problem. Dead, she could be forgotten. Then, in the eighth year of her death she came back. She was beautiful, but she had to die.

IN COLD PURSUIT
Ursula Curtiss

In Mexico, Mary and her cousin Jenny each encounter strange men, but neither of them realises that one of these men is obsessed with revenge and murder. But which one?